I0791926

Sweet Temptation

HONEYSUCKLE TEXAS ★ BOOK 3

CHRIS KENISTON

Indie House Publishing

Indie House Publishing

MORE BOOKS
By Chris Keniston

Honeysuckle Texas
Sweet Beginnings
Sweet Surprise
Sweet Temptation
Sweet Deal
Sweet Obsession
Sweet Tomorrows
Sweet Redemption

The Billionaire Barons of Texas
Just One Date
Just One Spark
Just One Dance
Just One Take
Just One Taste
Just One Shot
Just One Chance
Just One Mistake
Just One Family
Just One Rodeo
Just One Surprise
Just One Look

Hart Land
Heather
Lily
Violet
Iris
Hyacinth
Rose
Calytrix
Zinnia

Poppy
Picture Perfect

Farraday Country
Adam
Brooks
Connor
Declan
Ethan
Finn
Grace
Hannah
Ian
Jamison
Keeping Eileen
Loving Chloe
Morgan
Neil
Owen
Paxton
Quinn

Honeymoon Series
Honeymoon for One
Honeymoon for Three
Honeymoon for Four
Honeymoon for Five
Honeymoon for Six
Honeymoon for Seven

Aloha Romance Series:
Aloha Texas
Almost Paradise
Mai Tai Marriage
Dive Into You
Look of Love
Love by Design
Love Walks In
Shell Game
Flirting with Paradise

Surf's Up Flirts:
(Aloha Series Companions)
Shall We Dance
Love on Tap
Head Over Heels
Perfect Match
Just One Kiss
It Had to Be You
Cat's Meow

CHAPTER ONE

Checking his watch, Garret shoved the kitchen door open. Lingering scents of roast beef and fresh biscuits told him he wasn't too late for dinner. The familiar sounds of his family drifted from the dining room—Mason's excited chatter, Carson's measured responses, Jillian's gentle laughter, and, of course, his mother directing the evening. After a day of corralling seventh graders through the complexities of American history, followed by two hours of mending the fence line, all he wanted was food and his bed, in that order.

"There he is." His mom grinned up at him. "A little longer and I was going to send Brady to go find you."

The retired military dog, lounging at Mason's feet, barely lifted his head at the mention of his name.

"Sorry." Garret slid into his seat between Rachel and Preston. "I had a meeting after school with some parents that ran long and I'd told Clint that I would take care of the break in the fence by the east line that needed attention."

Rachel passed him the mashed potatoes. "You look dead on your feet."

"Says the woman who works day and night to save the world." Serving spoon in hand, he loaded his plate.

"To another day of the Sweet siblings burning the candle at both ends." Seated across from them, Jillian raised her water glass. "No pun intended."

That made just about everyone at the table chuckle. His sister Jillian's candle shop Heaven Scent had become one of the most popular shops on Main Street.

Garret dug into his food, the home-cooked meal a major step up from the sandwich he'd hastily swallowed hours ago between classes. At the head of the table, despite the financial tightrope everyone walked, his mother beamed at her assembled family. Preston and Carson's recent marriages had done a lot to ease some of the pressure, but there was still a long way to go. Since his sisters were having a hard time finding temporary spouses, and Kade was serving in the military overseas, the short straw, so to speak, fell to Garret. He needed to find a reasonable woman willing to play house with him—in name only, of course— sooner than later.

"Any sign of the horses?" Her plate empty, his mother dabbed at the corner of her mouth with the napkin. "Clint is wondering if maybe it's not the cattle, but the horses knocking down the fences."

"Could be." Preston nodded. "It would certainly explain why it's only become a problem recently."

The idea of the problem being wild horses and not decrepit fence posts sat much better with Garret. Especially since the ranch was still bleeding red ink. Big time.

"Your father would have loved having wild horses on the ranch." His mom chuckled to herself. "Well, until they tore down the first fence."

Again, the family around the table laughed with their mother. Chatter continued through dessert. Mason had grown restless and excused himself from the table, Brady faithfully following him. Until Mason arrived, Brady was their mother's keeper, but not anymore.

Pushing away from the table, Carson stood and came around to Garret's seat. "I'm heading upstairs to make sure Mason's getting started on his homework." He glanced up, waiting for his mom to carry her dishes into the kitchen, then leaned over, speaking softly. "Family meeting in Dad's study."

Garret nodded. That could only mean one thing. A financial update, or heaven forbid, a new problem.

"Nonnie." Jess came off the bottom step and swung around into the kitchen.

His mom had already popped her head out. "You rang?"

"You're being paged. Mason didn't have much

homework. Now he wants Nonnie to read him a story, or ten, before bed."

Smiling wider than the Cheshire Cat, their mom tossed the dishrag aside and hurried out of the kitchen and up the stairs.

One by one, the siblings and their spouses each filed into the study. The habit of gathering here to discuss the ranch happenings had become second nature.

"So, what's the story?" Jillian asked.

"Morning Glory," Rachel sang.

"What's the word," Sarah Sue chimed in.

To Garret's surprise, all three giggling, sang—loudly, "Hummingbird."

The three brothers looked to each other and then to the women now laughing like schoolgirls.

"What's the deal?" Preston asked from his seat at the desk.

"Don't you remember *Bye Bye Birdie*?" Rachel looked at him as if he'd forgotten his own birthday.

All three men shook their heads.

"How could you?" Jillian shook her head. "We only watched the movie about a hundred times over the years. You used to love the scene with Ann Margaret dancing."

Garret had to smile. His mother loved old movies and usually insisted her children suffer through them, but he had developed a bit of a crush on Ann Margaret from an early age. Still, whatever his sisters had just sung didn't ring any bells.

"Never mind." Sarah Sue sighed, her gaze directed at her husband. "Care to update?"

"The good news is the bank has stopped threatening to foreclose." Preston scrolled through something on the computer screen. "The bad news is we're still in the hole up to our necks and funds are stretched really thin."

"Darn shame the hay baler disappeared before we could sell it." Jess leaned against her husband.

Jillian nodded. "That would have helped raise some fast cash."

"Any new clues about who took it?" Rachel interjected.

"Nope." Preston swung his head left then right. "But the cameras haven't picked up any new strange activity, so there is that."

"I'll take any good news." Rachel leaned back in her seat, her one leg dangling over the arm of the chair, swinging like a pendulum.

"Then you won't want to hear this." Preston pulled a few pieces of paper from the printer. "This is our current financial picture. At the bottom you'll see what we still owe, what we're scheduled to pay at the end of the month, and how much we're short."

Garret let out a slow whistle. The numbers added up to more than he'd expected. The problem—and answer—were clear. They needed more money, a lot of it, and he needed to find someone soon to pass for his wife or things were going to go south fast. Very fast.

"You've completely lost your mind."

"I have not." Jackie Drake grabbed another shirt from the drawer and shoved it into the suitcase. "Once Brad understands that I'm willing to give up everything for him, that he doesn't have to ask me to leave behind my friends and home, he'll be over the moon."

"Hmm." Katie, her dearest friend since their sophomore year of college, pretty much thought Jackie should be committed. Of course, she'd never liked Brad. "Maybe you should just go for a short visit? See what it's like. If it doesn't work out, you can come home."

"Too late." She rolled another blouse. "Yesterday was my last day at work."

"What?" Katie's eyes almost fell out of her head. "You quit a job you love?"

"Gave my notice two weeks ago." Her favorite slippers went into the bag next. She didn't dare slow down, lest her closest friend see that she wasn't nearly as sure as she pretended to be. But her grandmother had always said believing was a verb, it required action, and she was definitely taking action.

"And you didn't tell me?"

Pausing, Jackie leveled her gaze with her bestie. "No, because you would have tried to talk me out of it." And she definitely didn't want that.

"Damn right I would have." Katie glanced around the one-bedroom apartment. "And this place?"

"I won't need it."

"You gave this up too?"

Jackie nodded. "Had to pay off the lease, but it's worth it."

Holding up both her hands, palms out, Katie shook her head and huffed like a bull about to charge. "And how much did that cost you?"

"Only three months' rent." She tried to make it sound like she hadn't had to clean out all her bank accounts to pay for the move.

"*Only*." Her bestie dropped her forehead into her hand and rubbed it very slowly before looking up again. "Jack, you know I want you to be happy."

"I will be. Brad's perfect."

"For what? The man is a poster boy for the modern playboy. He flirted with anything in a skirt no matter who was watching, who knows what he did when we weren't there to see."

"He's easily distracted." It was hard for a country boy in the city.

"Distracted? Are you listening to yourself? Breaking dates without calling is his MO. No man gets *that* lost in his work. Not to mention he's made it perfectly clear he doesn't want children."

Holding a lightweight sweater, she froze mid motion. "That's only because he hasn't been around them enough. I'm sure once we're married, he'll change his mind." Didn't her grandmother always say, if people waited till they were ready to have children, no one would have them?

"For the smartest woman I know," Katie fisted her hands on her hips, "you sure become a blithering idiot when it comes to Brad."

"Gee, thanks."

"Seriously. I want you to be happy, but with a nice guy who appreciates and cherishes you and wants to settle down and have a family. It's not like you're pushing forty or something. What's the hurry?"

"I'm not twenty anymore either. If I want to have the big family I've always dreamed of, Brad is my best option."

Katie sighed. "I'm not going to talk you out of this, am I?"

Shaking her head, she closed her suitcase. "Nope. And this is about it. What I don't wear anymore has either been dropped off at the consignment store or donated. I've already sold most of the kitchen things, and I have a few people coming by later today for some more of the furniture and odds and ends. What isn't gone by the time I leave tomorrow is going to be picked up by a local shelter."

"Lord love a duck." Katie rolled her eyes. "Jackie, please. Use your common sense. What are you going to do when you reach West Texas? Buy everything new with money you don't have?"

"I won't need anything. Brad's apartment was way nicer than this place, I'm sure wherever he's living in Millers Creek will be just as nice."

"Millers Creek. Sounds like a brewery. I don't like this—any of it."

"I know." Setting the bag down by the side of the bed, she smiled at her friend. "I appreciate how much you worry about me, but I'm okay. This will be good."

"Didn't your grandmother ever teach you there are plenty of fish in the sea? Why do you insist on hanging onto this slick eel of a guy?"

"He is not slick."

Katie merely raised a brow at her and sighed.

"He's charming, good-looking, well-educated, well employed, and we know we'll be perfectly happy together."

"We? Brad actually said this to you?" Katie crossed her arms.

"Well," she glanced down at the bag she'd just packed,

"not in those words."

"Uh-huh." Letting her arms fall to her side, Katie inched closer to her friend. "Please, tell me you at least have a backup plan if Brad doesn't work out."

She shook her head and grinned with more self-assurance than she felt. "Won't need one."

What she needed was to fly to Midland tomorrow, then drive to Millers Creek, and then she'd be reunited with Brad. So what if he had no idea she was coming? Doesn't everybody love surprises?

CHAPTER TWO

"W"here are you off to all dolled up?" Garret's sister Jillian paused in the hall by his bedroom door.

"Bronco Lounge."

"In Millers Creek?"

Buttoning his dress shirt, his fingers stilled and he turned to face his sister. "Is there another one I don't know of?"

"No." She shook her head. "But why are you going all the way to Millers Creek when the Whiskey Moon here in town is perfectly good for dancing and a drink."

"It is." He went back to buttoning his shirt. "But we already know everyone in town, and I don't know everyone in Millers Creek."

"And…?" Jillian's brows furrowed, waiting for more.

He tucked his shirt into his pressed jeans. "And I have to find a wife somewhere. Internet isn't working. In town wouldn't fly. So, I'm off to the Bronco Lounge."

"Yeah. I know what you mean." Jillian's head bobbed. "Maybe I should come too. Maybe there's some nice unattached man who isn't looking to get lucky."

"While there might be, going out with a woman might not be the best way for me to attract a potential bride."

"Of course." She blew out a deep sigh. "What do you think it would take to get as lucky as Carson and Preston?"

"A lifelong neighbor or a surprise baby?" He shrugged at her. "Sorry. This is just so much harder than it sounded when this idea first came up."

"At the time," Jillian leaned back against a dresser, "I thought Rachel was nuts, but it's worked out so far, it's just harder than I would have imagined to find cooperating males."

"Females too." He took a step back. "Okay. Ready or not. Unsuspecting bride, here I come."

Looking in the mirror one more time, Jackie ran her hands down the sides of her favorite dress. The color matched her eyes, and the fabric clung to curves in all the right places without looking too eager. Not that she needed spiffing up to get Brad's attention, but reminding him of what he was missing couldn't hurt.

Her purse in hand, she put the motel room key inside and spun about just for the heck of it. Today was going to be a great day. No matter what anyone said, she knew that the minute Brad saw her he'd remember all the good things, realize how much he missed her, and how easily they could make all their dreams a reality. Tomorrow, she'd move her bags to Brad's and start her happily ever after. Now, it was off to Brad's.

The clerk at the desk had told her that Millers Creek was once a key town in the cattle drive north. He'd claimed that the streets went every which way because that's where the cattle trails were. She had no idea if that was the truth or not, but she was very grateful for her GPS or she'd have never figured out what street went which way. Double-checking the house number and street name, she climbed into her car. Finding one of the change of address cards that Brad had filled out when he left Houston after losing his job and somehow accidentally wound up in her kitchen, was one of the things that had spurred her into action. With no real reason for the card to have gotten mingled with her mail, she took it as a sign. After adjusting the rearview mirror, she started the car, and hit go on the GPS.

A nice thing about small towns is even though Brad lived across town, it only took about fifteen minutes to get there. To her delight, the address wasn't an apartment, but a house. A cute little house with shutters and flower boxes and pretty red flowers. Who knew Brad had a domestic side? A sign that she was right. Brad would love family life once they were married.

Slinging her purse over her shoulder, she hopped out of the car, eager to see the look on Brad's face. Trying not to run, she followed the path to the front of the house. Taking in a deep breath, she rang the doorbell. Excitement effervesced inside her.

The door swung open, a long-haired blonde stood in the doorway, and confusion immediately stamped out her excitement.

"Yes?" the woman said.

"I'm sorry." Jackie did her best not to squirm. "I was looking for Brad Peters."

The woman smiled politely. "He's not home right now, but if you'll leave me your name, I'll let my husband know you stopped by."

Husband. Did she say husband? "I, uhm, that won't be necessary. I'll just give him a call another time."

"If you're sure?"

"I'm sure." She'd already started backing up, silently telling herself not to turn and run but walk slowly, casually, as if she were nothing more than a door to door solicitor and Brad Peters was just a stranger.

Climbing into the car as fast as she could, she started the engine, and without her GPS, just drove. How had this happened? How had she not realized there was another woman, never mind a wife? Handsome and charming, she'd been flattered when he'd noticed her. Later, he'd been so attentive, never looking at his phone when they were together. She'd thought it showed how much he cared, but he was probably just worried his wife would call. All those nights that he'd insisted they stay home, curled up on the sofa, watching old movies. Again she'd thought he cared too much to share her with the world. What a fool she'd been. She couldn't call Katie, not to hear I told you so. Tears pressing against her eyeballs threatened to overflow. Swiping at the corners, a horn honked and a car flew past her. Glancing up, she'd run a red light. Lord, wouldn't that just be the perfect end to a horrible turn of events? She had no job, no place to live, no one to turn to, and no money.

Turning into the first parking lot entrance she found, she pulled over and shutting off the engine, stared at the blinking neon light ahead. The tears came in earnest. Leaning on the steering wheel, Jackie let them flow. What the hell had she done to her life?

From Garret's first sight of the blinking neon Bronco Lounge sign, he considered turning around. He had to be insane coming to a pick-up joint to find a wife, even a temporary one. On the other hand, looking for a temporary wife could be considered insane in and of itself, so maybe looking for one here wasn't as crazy as it felt. At least he was going to keep telling himself that.

Taking a deep breath, he yanked the bar door open and the heat of bodies jammed together in the small club slapped him in the face. One foot in front of the other, he pushed forward, reminding himself of the six-digit number that they still needed to save the ranch.

The dance floor was completely packed. With every table and booth filled, the bar was standing room only. Maybe it wasn't the best idea coming here. Determined to at least give this a try, he squeezed in at the bar, waiting for the bartender to have a free moment. While waiting, a man paid his tab and walked away, and Garret swiftly grabbed the seat.

From where he sat, he had a perfect view of almost the whole place. Slowly sipping his beer, he took note of the people coming and going, particularly the female ones. A pretty brunette caught his eye. Unlike most of the women, she wasn't all gussied up, just seemed to be herself. Unfortunately for him, a cowboy came into the place, and the way the brunette lit up and threw her arms around his neck, Garret was going to have to keep looking.

A lovely blonde sitting alone in the corner, nursing a drink, with two empty glasses beside her, caught his interest. She seemed to not just be alone, but lonely. Not once had he noticed her look up, she just stared down at the drink, swirling the straw around. A redhead came up to him and smiling wryly, she offered to buy him a drink. As tempted as he was to say yes, something told him she wasn't what he was looking for. Apologizing, he flirted with the truth, telling her he was waiting for someone. No reason to let her know he had no idea who that was or if she would turn up.

Looking to the corner, the blonde was gone. The door opened and closed, more people strolling in, mostly couples walking out, though he had his doubts many of them had arrived together. Laughter from the dance floor had him looking the other way. The blonde's mood had shifted, probably with the help of the three, or more, drinks she's consumed. She was dancing around, bouncing back and forth like a pinball, not quite dancing with anyone in particular. Though one man seemed to be especially interested in her… moves.

"Lonely, cowboy?" a petite gal in skin-tight jeans asked.

He thought he'd scoped out every female in the place, he must have missed this one. Knowing he couldn't say no to everyone, he smiled, said something simple and spent the next thirty minutes wishing he'd told her he was waiting for someone.

She swallowed the last sip of her wine and grinned at him. "Wanna dance?"

No was probably not the right answer. "Sure."

Every time she reached for his hand, or arm, or whatever, Garret spun in the other direction. Who knew having learned to maneuver on the football field would help on the dance floor? Just as he swung around the opposite direction of the redhead, his hip bumped into someone.

To his surprise, the blonde stumbled back, almost falling over. Garret reached out, taking hold of her arms until she was balanced on her own, sort of.

"Sorry." She paused a long moment and leveled her gaze with his. Despite the smile on her face, her eyes told a totally different story.

He hadn't seen that kind of pain in a woman's eyes since his dad died. Never would he forget the look in his mom's eyes when Doc Conroy told her she had lost her husband.

A new tune he didn't recognize played overhead and throwing her arms up in the air, the blonde began singing at the top of her lungs, shimmying about the floor as if she were the only person here.

Not sure what to make of it, he turned to the redhead and to his delight, noticed she'd grown interested in another guy. About to offer to buy the blonde something a little sobering, like a cup of coffee, she bumped into another guy who didn't hesitate to grab her and twirl her into a close dance move. Maybe she knew the guy.

Time to go back to his observation post, except now, his seat at the bar was gone. Opting to just stand by the corner, he soon grew tired of watching the people coming and going in hopes of finding a potential prospect for an absurd bargain. Instead, he opted to watch the pretty blonde, dancing with yet another man.

If he were placing bets, there'd be two choices, a bachelorette having a little too much fun, except there were no bridesmaids about and the sadness he'd seen in her eyes told him the other choice was more likely. A break-up. And from the way she was dancing, spilling the drink she held high in the air, he'd venture it was a bad break up. A real lulu. What he didn't know was if she knew anyone here at all. Most likely, since seeing her at the table a few hours ago all by herself, probably not.

A new guy appeared at the blonde's side. Apparently, Garret wasn't the only one watching the woman. This guy looked slick, and cool, and like he had only one thing on his mind. Sure enough, dancing with her, he pulled the clip from her hair, and when she laughed, shaking out long blonde locks that fell past her shoulders, the guy dared to tug at her strap and expose a soft, shoulder that hadn't seen sunshine in a long time.

Acid churned in his stomach. Sure people came into places like this looking for companionship, especially the kind that didn't include names or staying for breakfast, but there were rules about girls who'd had too much to drink, and this girl—this woman—definitely fell into that category. Any idiot could see she'd lost control of her good sense a long time ago.

Part of him tried to tell himself that she wasn't his responsibility, he wasn't her keeper. Then the other part of him asked, what if that were Jillian or Rachel, would he want someone to step in and save her from herself?

As he continued silently debating, another guy came up to the blonde. Now the two guys were after her—at the same time—and then, for just a second he saw a flash of, was it fear, before she let out a nervous laugh and danced with both men.

That was it. Saving her from herself, from throwing her life away, was his responsibility, at least tonight.

CHAPTER THREE

Marching over, Garret insinuated himself between the blonde and the first guy. "Come on…" Crud, he had no idea what her name was, then again, these two yahoos probably didn't know it either. "Mary, it's time to go home." Taking hold of her arm as delicately as he could while still forcing a woman to go with a man she'd never met before in her life, he looked her in the eyes and prayed she could see he had no untoward intent.

"Wh…at…" she slurred.

Oh, definitely time to save her from herself. "We're going home."

"Home?" For the first time since he'd been watching her, he saw the hint of a genuine smile.

"Yes. Home."

She almost melted against him, though she may have been on the verge of passing out. With no choice, he looped his arm around her waist and started moving forward when one of the two bozos grabbed his arm.

"Hey man, she's with us."

Garret gave the man a glare that should have cut him to his knees. Thankfully, it worked; not one but both of the men retreated.

He'd barely made it across the room to the door when one of the waitresses came running up to them. "Honey, don't forget your purse."

Purse. Thank heaven for that. He was about to walk off with a woman he didn't know, and take her who knew where.

"Thanks." He nodded at the woman.

Outside, she gasped at the fresh air and then wobbled

beside him. Not sure quite what to do now, he took her to his car. Settling her in the front seat, he opened her purse and muttering an apology, ignored her phone—most were locked with a pass code—instead, he pulled out her wallet. Jacqueline. Such a pretty name. He took a second to look at the woman squinting at him.

"That's mine."

"Yes, it is. Jacqueline."

She leaned her head back and smiled. "My mom loooved, Jackie……Ken, kennnn."

"Kennedy?" he finished for her, looking back at her license for an address. *Houston*? What the heck was a gal from Houston doing in a dive like this in the heart of a small West Texas town? "Jacqueline, where do you live now?"

"Home," she muttered softly, her eyes drifting closed.

"That's right. Where is home?"

Nothing.

"Jacqueline?"

No response. Marvelous. Going back to her purse, he searched for something else. A key fob from a car rental agency. Holding it up, he clicked the fob. Nothing. She might have been parked too far away. Didn't matter. She was in no condition to drive, and where was he going to take the car and her anyhow? One more scan. What was it about a woman's purse that gave every man on the planet the heeby jeebies. The odds of a rattle snake biting him were beyond impossible, and yet, a woman's purse was a mysterious world he really wished he didn't have to rummage through. Noticing a thin pocket, he unzipped it and bingo. A hotel key. Or motel. But where?

The downside of modern technology was that the generic cards rarely had a hotel name or room number. The upside, of course, was that lost keys couldn't lead to burglaries. Neither of which helped at the moment. So, the question facing him was: now what?

Fighting to open her eyes, Jackie wondered when her arms got so heavy. Doing her best to lift her head, the slightest movement made her stomach roll. What the hell had she done to herself?

Blinking, the neon sign shone down on her. She was dancing. Drinking. Trying to forget. Forget that the man she'd hung all her dreams on had actually been her worst nightmare. "Married."

"What?" a male voice sounded close. Very close. "Jacqueline, what hotel are you staying at?"

Jacqueline. Was she in trouble?

"Do you know the name of the hotel?" The voice was low and deep and patient.

"Brad?"

"No. Where are you staying?"

Of course it wasn't Brad. His voice might have been smooth as carrera marble, but there was nothing patient about it. "Wife," she muttered.

"Should I call Brad?" that same voice asked. "Do you have a phone number?"

No. She didn't have Brad, she didn't have anything. Nothing. Her eyes were so heavy. She couldn't move her legs. How was she going to dance if she couldn't move her legs?

Out cold. Again. No matter how hard Garret tried, there was no way Jacqueline was going to sober up soon enough to tell him where she lived. All he could do was hope that if she was Brad's wife, the guy was going to appreciate Garret saving her and not kill him. Though what he'd like to know is what had this character done to her to send her off to a drunken escape in a pick-up joint like Bronco's.

Placing her purse in her lap, he fastened her seat belt for her and closed the door. He didn't have much choice. His phone in hand, he texted his sisters Rachel and Jillian, to let them know he wouldn't be home tonight. Knowing neither kept their phones by their beds so he wouldn't wake them, at least no one would worry in the morning.

Driving through town, he pulled into the first decent motel he came across. Leaning over, even though she was out cold, he told Jacqueline he'd be right back.

It took about ten minutes to pay for two rooms and return to the car. Driving around the building to the appropriate numbers, he parked. Realizing she wasn't going to be in any shape to move on her own steam, or maybe even stand on her own steam, he opted to unlock and open her room door first.

The room open, he hurried back to the car, opened the door, unclasped the seat belt. "Jacqueline?"

Nothing. Not a blink, not a mumble, nothing.

"We're at the motel. You need to get up." He knew she wasn't going to respond, but he had to try before helping her out.

No surprise, she was pretty much dead weight. Sliding her legs out of the car, he tried not to notice how shapely they were. Even though it had been obvious to everyone at Bronco's that she had an hourglass figure, he still tried not to think about it. Tugging her to her feet, she almost fell against him. It was clear he was going to have to help. Slipping his arm around her back and the other under her knees, scooped her up into his arms and walked her to the room.

Inside, he kicked the door shut and carried her to the bed. Gently laying her down, he took off her shoes, then went hunting through the closet and pulled out a spare blanket to spread over her. Convinced she was as comfortable as he could make her—short of stripping her out of her clothes to tuck her in, and he was most definitely not going there—he went back to the car and grabbed her purse.

Setting it and her car key fob on the dresser, next he went in search of paper and pen.

He scribbled a brief note hoping it didn't sound too stalkerish and left it by her purse and keys, and pulling the door tightly behind him, left her to sleep. Alone.

Inside his own room, he tossed his keys on the dresser and emptied his pockets. Kicking off his shoes, he settled on the bed. In no mood to climb under the covers, he merely threaded his hands behind his head and stared up at the ceiling.

In the room behind him, through the paper-thin wall, he could hear the person coughing away. Probably a smoker. That or the person had no business being away from home.

Thinking back on his night, he chuckled softly to himself. This was not what he'd planned for his evening out. One more failed effort at finding a one-year wife to help keep the ranch. But at least there was one thing he felt good about; he'd rescued a drunk girl from a bad situation, and now she was in her room, sleeping, alone.

CHAPTER FOUR

Sunshine streamed into the room like a laser beam in the dark. Normally, Jackie would love a bright sunny day, but right now, a carpenter was pounding a rapid succession of hammer strikes somewhere near her head.

Opening one eye, she could see there was no carpenter nearby and the banging wasn't in the room, it was in her head. Right between her eyes. And against her temples. Was that even possible? Had she ever felt this miserable in her entire life?

What the heck had she done to herself? A car accident? A fall? Was she in a hospital? Forcing her eyes to open fully, she stared at the ceiling. Any effort to turn her head only managed to add a stabbing pain to the already-splitting headache, but if she wanted to piece together what was happening, she'd have to look around. Gently turning her head to the left, she searched for IVs or nurses, or something to explain the shooting pains in her head.

Nothing. Except, where the heck was she? Nothing about this room seemed familiar. All she could decipher is that she was in a hotel. A hotel? Rubbing at the left side of her temple, she tried to remember how she got here. Nothing. Maybe if she thought on the last thing she could remember. She was leaving Houston. She'd sold or donated most of her belongings and quit her job to join Brad in West Texas. *Brad.* That's right.

She'd flown to Midland, rented a car and couldn't wait to see the look of surprise on his face when she showed up on his doorstep. She'd checked into a motel. Glancing around again, she thought hard on the motel. Definitely not this one. Which brought her back to, how did she get here?

Panic began to roil in her stomach, an unexpected urge to heave had her rolling onto her side despite the hammering in her head. Staying perfectly still, she waited for the unease to pass. The need to upchuck gone—for now—she replayed recent events in her head. She'd left the motel in her most knock-your-socks-off dress and headed for the address she had for Brad.

It was all starting to come back to her. She'd been so excited. Surprised by how cute the house was—and then she remembered, the bigger surprise was learning Brad had a wife. *A wife*. She'd backed away as fast as she could and had a good cry. Then she'd decided what she really needed was a stiff drink. How many had she had? So much made sense now. Why he traveled so often, why he'd always told her his time in Houston was temporary, why he cut her off completely, why he didn't want to start a family with her— he already had one.

Scrubbing her hands down her face, the light seemed a tad less offensive, even though the hammering was still banging away in her head. The need to pee forced her out of the bed. Slowly, unsteadily, but out. Her mind continued to replay the events of last night. She'd cried. A lot. Noticed the sign for the club. Something Lounge. A drink and maybe a dance or two would be better than going back to an empty motel room and wallowing over what a major mess she'd made of her life in just a few short weeks. When had she become so stupid? So blinded by the rapid ticking of her biological clock that she'd latched on to the only viable contender for life partner she'd found.

She'd hoped splashing a little water on her face would help wake her up and bring clarity to the situation. All it did was get her wet. She should go back to bed.

Wobbling over to the bed, extending a hand against the wall every few feet to stabilize herself, she stopped midway. What good would going back to bed do? She was going to have to face her new reality sooner or later. If only the hammering would stop. Where was her purse? She had ibuprofen in there. Right about now she figured half a bottle should do the trick. The question at hand; where *was* her purse? Probably the same place as her memory of last night.

Scanning the room, she spotted her purse and her keys on the dresser a few feet ahead. One slow and unsteady step at a time, she crept over, dug out the pain meds, and watched a sheet of paper drift to the floor.

Water, she needed water to swallow the pills. Turning around, she retraced her steps to the bathroom, popped three pills into her mouth and then cupped the water, bringing it to her face and swallowing the pain relief meds. She only hoped it worked.

In the mirror she could see the bags under her eyes, probably from a lack of sleep. Her dress was the same from last night, the one guaranteed to make Brad trip over his tongue. Where were her pajamas? Looking around, where were her clothes? Her suitcase? And why was she here? Squeezing her eyes, she just couldn't remember what happened after she'd walked into the club, ordered a drink, and sat alone at a table. Yes, she was alone. At first.

Lord, she was so confused. Making her way back to the bed, her gaze drifted to the paper on the ground. Had that been in her purse? Was it here when she checked in? No point in asking herself questions she couldn't answer. She leaned over, immediately regretting the roil in her stomach and shooting pain between her eyes, and snatched hold of the sheet of paper, straightened, and squinted to read.

Jacqueline,

I brought you here from Bronco's Lounge because I didn't know where you live.

If you need a ride to your car – call me at 432-555-2236 –

If not, take care,
Garret Sweet

That's right. The flashing sign was for the Bronco Lounge. But who was Garret? Did she need him to give her a ride? Would it matter if he saw her in the same dress as last night? Last night? Her breath caught in her chest, her mouth dropped open and her eyes widened. Good grief, surely she hadn't. She couldn't have. Could she? No, if anything had happened between her and Garret, wouldn't he still be here instead of leaving her a note?

Definitely no. Whoever this person was, the note sounded like nothing more than a concerned citizen. After all, if there had been a one nightstand, the guy would have run as far and fast as he could. Now she had a new question to ask herself—should she call and get a ride to her car?

If Garret had gotten an hour's sleep last night, it was a lot. The people in the room behind his headboard had hacked up a lung well into the early morning hours, and the room with Jacqueline had been completely silent. Until now.

At first he wasn't sure where the footsteps had come from, but then he heard a toilet flush, water run, and more footsteps. She was awake. He'd wait for her to have enough time to read the note, then if she didn't need a ride to her car, he'd go home to his chores. Walk away and never think back on the woman in the next room.

What he didn't know, was how long was long enough. Glancing at the old-fashioned alarm clock on the nightstand, it was a little after ten in the morning. Less than an hour until check out. That's what he would do, wait till it was time to check out. That was reasonable. Of course, since he'd never had to take a perfect stranger home without any clue of where she lived, who knew what was reasonably a long enough wait.

Wishing he had a toothbrush, he pushed up from the bed, headed for the bathroom, rinsed his mouth out with water, and finger combed his hair. It would have to do. A light rapping on the door startled him. Was it her? Maybe it was a maid, wanting to clean the room. Or someone warning him of upcoming check out time. Or perhaps he should just open the door and find out.

Taking larger than usual strides, he pulled the door open.

Her eyes not fully open, Jacqueline seemed to be focusing on his face. Or thinking.

He wasn't quite sure. "Morning."

"Oh." Now her eyes were wide open. "Good morning."

"Would you like to come in?" He stepped to one side and opened the door enough for her to easily enter the room.

"Actually." She seemed to be considering her words carefully. "I checked with the front desk about my bill. They said it was paid and that you had the room next to mine." Her gaze dropped a moment before she found the nerve to look him in the eye again. "I'm here to take you up on that offer to pick up my car."

"Oh, yes. Sure. Of course." Crossing the room in a few long strides, he grabbed his keys from the nightstand and slid into his loafers. Turning and dangling the keys in the air, he smiled. "Let's go."

The smile must have been the right thing to do. For a second, surprise flashed in her eyes just before her own slight smile teased at her lips. "Thank you."

Settled in the car, unlike last night, she easily managed to snap her seat belt in place. Hands folded in her lap, her gaze remained fixed on the road. Hands resting in her lap like an obedient schoolgirl shouldn't be enough, but everything about her timid and quiet behavior screamed at him that she was what his Gramma Davis would call a good girl. That made him glad he'd done what he'd done. Taken the chance he'd taken bringing her, not exactly against her will, but definitely without her consent.

"Is it far?" she dared to glance in his direction. "My car?"

He shook his head. "Millers Creek is bigger than Honeysuckle, but not by much."

"Honeysuckle?"

"The town where I live. Little less than an hour away as the crow flies."

"Ah."

The first red light seemed to be interminable. So much so that he actually wondered if it might be broken. At the same moment the light changed, Jacqueline's stomach grumbled.

Immediately, her hand flattened against her. "Sorry."

"No need, but I could stand a little food myself. Care to join me for breakfast?" His gaze shifted to the clock on the dashboard. "Okay, brunch."

Her shoulders relaxed. "I think that would be nice."

"Great." He was almost surprised at how pleased he was that she'd agreed. "There's a nice little place across the street from where we left your car."

"Good plan."

It only took a few more minutes to pull into the Cracked Egg parking lot. The car in park, he rounded the hood and reached her door before she could shove it open herself.

"Thank you." Her smile was dim, but at least it wasn't a fearful frown.

Inside, the hostess led them to a booth near the far corner of the place. A few heads turned in their direction; they were definitely a bit overdressed for the time of day.

Her nose buried in the menu, Garret took the time to observe her freely. She was prettier than he remembered, or maybe it was just the light of day that showed her beauty. That almost made him laugh, one good deed and he was waxing poetic.

"Need some time or ready to order?" The waitress stood over them, a pad in her hand, while another person set two glasses of water in front of them.

"Are you ready?" he asked.

Jacqueline nodded. "Yes, I'll have a cheese and spinach omelet, a side of bacon, two blueberry pancakes, no toast, and a glass of orange juice."

If nothing else, the woman had a healthy appetite. Fortunately for him, working on a ranch kept him burning the carbs. "I'll have the same."

The two glasses of juice arrived first. Jacqueline took her first sip and Garret tried not to stare.

"I want to apologize."

"For what?" He reached for his glass.

"Whatever I did last night."

"Whatever?" No wonder she was so quiet, she didn't remember.

"I, uh, don't remember much after ordering a drink and sitting down."

"There's a good reason for that."

Her eyes lit up. "There is?"

"Sorry, but as my grandmother used to say, you were three sheets to the wind."

"I figured as much. I don't usually have more than a glass of wine. Two if it's a really long dinner with a lot of food."

"I see." He nodded. "Want to tell me what happened?"

Fiddling with the paper napkin, she twirled it between her fingers.

"You don't have to. We can just eat."

"I was an idiot."

Not what he was expecting to hear.

"I gave up everything—my apartment, my job, most of my belongings—to follow a man."

Somehow, that didn't surprise him. "He wasn't happy to see you?"

"I wouldn't know." Now both hands worried the napkin. "His wife answered the door."

"Ouch." He hadn't meant to say that out loud. "Sorry."

"No." She nodded. "That about says it all. After I cried my eyes out in the parking lot, too embarrassed to call my friend, too mortified to go home, especially when I thought about not having anything to go home to, a glass of wine and a few dances sounded like a good idea. Something to get my mind off what a mess I've made of my life."

"What's that expression, it's always darkest before the dawn? I'm sure you'll work it all out."

"Glad someone is."

He didn't like the frown that settled softly between her brows. "Don't you have family you can turn to?"

She shook her head. "My parents divorced when I was a toddler. Mom raised me on her own for a while and then moved in with my grandparents. By the time I was ten, Mom left and we never heard from her again. My grandparents didn't have much, but they took good care of me, gave me lots of love. I moved away after graduating college. My grandfather died shortly thereafter, but Gramma is a rock. She still sends me care packages of baked goods." Her gaze softened and a smile teased her lips. "Just in case I'm not eating well."

"That's sweet."

She nodded, her somber expression returning. "I can't go back like this with my unemployed and brokenhearted tail between my legs."

"I'm sorry." What more could he say? His Grandma Davis died at least a decade ago and every once in a while, a wave of missing her would catch him by surprise, but he would have done anything to avoid disappointing that sweet old lady.

She sat back as the server set their meals on the table. Between bites, he told her about growing up with five siblings, how the twins, the babies of the family, had everyone wrapped around their finger. Reminiscing had kept him smiling through the meal.

"I really do—sorry, *did*—love my job, but I have to admit, I wasn't fond of Houston. I grew up in Tyler, East Texas, and Houston is hot, and muggy, and humid, and rainy, and soggy, and crowded, and it feels like we live on the freeways, stuck in traffic."

He laughed. "Why don't you tell me how you really feel?"

"Oh, I can be quite opinionated when I'm not feeling foolish, and a bit embarrassed."

"There's nothing wrong with following your heart. I know it seems awful now, but maybe this is for the best, getting you out of Houston."

"Maybe." Though she didn't look convinced.

The server encouraged them to try the Boston cream pie special.

"Oh, my. This is good." Jacqueline stabbed at the pie with unexpected gusto.

"You'd get along with my sister Rachel."

Her gaze lifted to meet his. "I would?"

"Yeah, she has that same fervor for life...and pie... as you seem to."

"Thank you." Using her fork to poke at the pie on her plate, she didn't look up. "Is there a lot of work in Honeyville?"

"Honeysuckle. And it depends on what you do, but we're growing. New businesses are coming to town, and so are the tourists with all the festivals."

"Festivals?"

"The corn hole championship is the longest and busiest one, but we have more. Folks like gathering to celebrate pretty much anything."

"Sounds nice."

"I think so." Finishing up, he closed his knife and fork, and set his napkin down beside his empty plate. "You planning on staying here for a while?"

She shrugged. "I'm not sure what I'm going to do, but at least I've remembered the name of my motel."

"Hey," he grinned at her, "that's progress."

To his surprise, she actually chuckled. "I guess it is." Lifting her water glass in a mock toast, she waited for him to do the same. "To progress."

"Progress." Taking a sip and looking at her over the rim of his glass, all he could think was, what a shame they hadn't met at a different place or time. Really a shame.

CHAPTER FIVE

oneysuckle, Texas had to be the quaintest little place Jackie had ever seen. Nostalgia oozed from every storefront on Main Street—from the hardware store with its red-and-white striped awning to the beauty salon with the hand-painted sign. She'd been on the road to Midland, resigned to returning to Houston and facing Katie's "I told you so" and the humiliating job hunt that awaited her, when thoughts of Garret's easy smile, the warmth in his voice when he'd mentioned the festivals and the growing town, and the love in his eyes when he spoke of his family and the ranch, prompted her to pull off to the side of the road and type in Honeysuckle, Texas. The town was only an hour away from the freeway. When the exit came, curiosity drove her to follow through. Just a quick look, she told herself, delaying the inevitable return to reality.

Now, here she was wandering the length of Main Street, sipping a lemonade and working up the nerve to get in her car and drive to Midland to return the rental. From there, she'd head to her final destination, Houston. Of course, with no place to live and little money, her only option was to land on her friend's sofa and start her life over again.

A slight breeze carried the sound of laughter from the park at the edge of town before Main Street turned into homes and tree-lined streets. Jackie followed it, finding herself on a foot path that led to an open green space with picnic tables, swings, and smack dab in the middle of a group of children playing, from where she stood, what looked like a game of corn hole. Though she'd seen bocce courts, basketball courts, and even tennis courts in neighborhood parks, this was a first for corn hole.

Then she remembered, Garret had told her that Honeysuckle was the corn hole capital of Texas. Now the park made sense.

"That's a mighty fine toss, young lady!" A smiling woman clapped enthusiastically.

"Thanks, Miss Vicki!" The girl beamed, skipping back to retrieve her bags.

Jackie settled on a bench, watching the game. It looked simple enough—toss the bag into the hole. The children were surprisingly skilled, high-fiving after successful tosses. So this was corn hole. Everything here was so simple, so sweet, so Norman Rockwell. No wonder Garret spoke so fondly of his hometown.

The thought of Garret brought warmth to her cheeks. She'd spent far too much time thinking about him since their breakfast two days ago. He'd been kind when she'd needed kindness most, and hadn't judged her lowest moment. And most importantly, he'd saved her from herself when no one else would.

Jackie's hand drifted to her purse, fingers seeking the note she should have thrown away but hadn't. The creases were already soft from repeated folding and unfolding. She wasn't even sure why she'd kept it. Maybe because it represented someone doing something decent for her with no expectations.

"Do you play?"

Jackie jumped, looking up at the woman who had been cheering the children. Shading the sun from her eyes with her hand, she smiled. "Can't say that I ever have?"

"That explains the look."

"The look?"

"A little bit fascination mixed with moments of confusion." The woman settled beside her on the bench. "Vicki Langley. My sister Liz and I own Corn Hole Heaven just up the street."

"Jackie Drake. And yes, it's my first time seeing the game played. It looks fun."

"Fun? Honey, it's a religion around here." Vicki chuckled. "Stop by the shop if you'd like to learn more.

We've got the best selection of boards, bags, and accessories in the state."

"I might just do that."

Vicki patted her knee. "You visiting or passing through?"

"Just passing through. I was in Millers Creek, but…" Jackie hesitated. "Things didn't work out."

"Ah." Vicki nodded knowingly. "Well, Honeysuckle's a better town anyway. Friendlier."

"So I've heard." The familiar weight of uncertainty settled in Jackie's chest. "I should really get back on the road soon."

"Where you headed?"

"Houston via Midland Odessa airport."

Vicki made a face. "That concrete jungle? You sure?"

Nodding, Jackie laughed despite herself. Right now she wasn't sure of anything, but Houston held more options than returning to East Texas.

"Well, before you go, you should at least see Corn Hole Heaven. And our niece's candle shop, Heaven Scents, is just a few doors down. Jillian makes the finest scented candles in the state."

A small tussle amongst the children broke out and Vicki jumped to her feet. "Oops, I'm supposed to be teaching the kids how to improve their game, and, of course, be good sports about winning or losing. Clearly, I'm falling down on the job. I need to run, but remember to stop by the shops before you leave town."

Jackie nodded.

"And if you're thinking of staying, there's a help wanted bulletin board at the café. Agnes will show you where."

Smiling, Jackie nodded at the woman as she returned to the children, her mind turning over the crazy idea of staying a little longer. She didn't have a job, or much money, and credit cards could only get you so far without a job or money.

Fingering the note in her purse once more, she couldn't decide if popping into the café would be a good or bad idea.

Then again, she was getting pretty good at bad ideas, what was one more?

Navigating the hallway crowded with students rushing for the exits, Garret checked his watch for the third time. Three-thirty. If he could get to his truck within five minutes, he might actually make it to the south pasture to lend Carson and Preston a hand in repairing that irrigation line before dinner.

"Mr. Sweet!" A seventh-grader skidded to a halt in front of him. "I forgot to turn in my permission slip for the museum trip."

Garret suppressed a sigh. "Come on back to the classroom, Mikey."

Five minutes turned into fifteen as he sorted out Mikey's paperwork, then answered an urgent email from the principal about next week's parent-teacher conferences. By the time he finally made it to the parking lot, he was already mentally calculating how much time they'd have left for repairs.

Sliding into his truck, he tossed his bag onto the passenger seat and started the engine. The truck rumbled to life just as his phone buzzed. A text from Carson: *Irrigation line not as bad as we thought. Don't rush.*

Well, that was something at least. Garret pulled out of the school lot, turning toward Main Street. He could use a coffee for the drive home, and Agnes made the best in town.

As he cruised past the town park, something—or rather someone—caught his eye. A flash of blonde hair, a familiar profile. He slowed the truck, squinting through the passenger window.

It couldn't be.

But it was. Jackie Drake, looking far less hungover and much more at ease in a pair of slacks and t-shirt than she had the last time he'd seen her. Near the edge of the corn hole courts, she snapped her purse shut and stood.

Before he could think better of it, feeling an urgent need to hurry before she slipped away, Garret pulled into a parking space and cut the engine. What were the odds? He'd been unable to get her out of his mind for the past two days, wondering if she'd found a solution to her predicament. More than once he'd wished that he'd gotten her phone number, but at the time, he hadn't thought she'd be so hard to forget.

Hurriedly, he crossed the street, hands in his pockets, suddenly uncertain. She hadn't noticed him yet, her attention focused on some distant point down the street. The sunlight caught in her hair, highlighting strands of gold among the blonde. She looked different here—less lost, more curious.

"Fancy meeting you here," he called from the curb.

Jackie whirled around, surprise widening her eyes before a smile spread across her face. "Hi."

Had he ever been so happy to see a woman smile? Closing the distance between them, he returned the smile. "What brings you to Honeysuckle?"

She tucked a strand of hair behind her ear, a faint blush coloring her cheeks. "I was on my way to return the rental in Midland, but then I remembered what you said about the town and thought I should take a look for myself since it's unlikely I'll ever be out this way again."

"Yeah, well," he glanced down the street, "I hope it lived up to your expectations."

"Far beyond. It's everything you said it was." She looked over her shoulder at his aunt and the children. "I got distracted watching the children playing. That nice lady came to talk to me for a few minutes. Like you said, Honeysuckle is friendlier than Millers Creek."

"Glad Aunt Vicki made you feel welcome."

Surprise clung to her face. "That's your aunt?"

He nodded. "Yep. And one of those kids over there is my nephew Mason."

"That explains her indoctrination in the local religion."

"Definitely sounds like you've been chatting with our local corn hole evangelist." Garret couldn't hold back his amusement. "Her and Aunt Liz could convert anyone to corn hole."

"She's sweet." Jackie smiled. "Invited me to visit their shop and the candle shop, and the café."

"What, she left out the ice cream parlor and beauty salon?"

"There wasn't enough time." Jackie laughed, pointing to his aunt and the kids. "The natives were growing restless."

He glanced at her grip on her purse strap. "Were you about to leave?"

"Oh, well, actually, I was thinking of stopping at the café first."

"Really," he tried not to grin like a cat with a belly full of cream, "I was just going that way for a cup of Agnes's coffee before I head to the ranch."

"Oh." Her gaze darted down the street and back.

"Would you care to join me for a cup, maybe a bite to eat?"

Her hesitation almost had him backpedaling the offer before she smiled and nodded. "That would be nice."

"So." Walking the short distance to the café, he kept his hands in his pockets resisting an odd urge to hold her hand. "What did you think of our little town?"

"It's charming. Very different from Houston. Or Millers Creek, for that matter."

"Born and raised here. It grows on you. Even after leaving for college, I had to come back. Couldn't imagine living anywhere else." Reaching the café, he opened the door and waved her in, not at all surprised by all the heads that turned to face them. Clearly, his aunt hadn't had time to spread the word an available female was in town.

Agnes hurried over, two menus in hand. "Always nice to see you, Garret Sweet. Staying or take out?"

"Staying. We'll take a table."

"All I have are booths." Without waiting Agnes turned on her heel and walking past a couple of open spots, led them to the last booth in the place. By tomorrow, tongues would be wagging. What he didn't know was if that would turn out to be a good or bad thing.

CHAPTER SIX

Seated with her back to the rest of the patrons, Jackie tried not to think about all the people who might be watching them.

"Don't let them unsettle you." Garret smiled.

"Them?" She brushed at a nonexistent piece of dust on the tabletop. "Is it that obvious?"

"That you noticed the place staring at us as we walked in? Or that it made you nervous?"

She shrugged. "Both, I guess."

"I teach junior high, when something is obvious, it's easier to just go with it."

This man was so relaxed and easy-going, that no matter how off kilter she might feel, he seemed to be able to put her at ease. Or maybe two meals together wasn't enough to draw such sweeping conclusions and her observations were nothing more than wishful thinking. The same wishful thinking that had gotten her in trouble with Brad.

"When do you leave for Houston?"

Jackie hesitated. Should she share that she'd actually been thinking about looking on that bulletin board for work in town? "I need to return the car to the airport tomorrow. I was supposed to return it in Millers Creek since I thought, well, you know what I thought."

He nodded but didn't speak.

"But I couldn't bring myself to actually buy a ticket to Houston, so I'll probably hop on the next available flight after I return the car. Maybe Midland will be more interesting than I remember and I'll stick around a bit." She forced a relaxed smile. "Or, who knows, maybe I'll wind up someplace exotic, like Paris."

"I sure hope you don't mean Paris, Texas."

"No," she laughed in earnest, "I don't. But I've pretty much reached my limit on spontaneous adventures. Like it or not, it will be a flight to Houston. I just hate admitting defeat. And boy did I bomb."

"Some people might consider your new perspective on life a chance at a fresh start. Even in Houston."

She was right. It wasn't just coincidence. The man had a way of making things feel better. "Somehow it would feel fresher if I weren't starting out with my tail between my legs and sleeping on a friend's sofa. Not exactly starting from a position of strength."

"You're stronger than you think."

Wow. After all he'd seen her do, all he knew she'd done, did he really think of her as strong?

Before he could say anything else, Agnes came up to them with a couple of glasses of water, silverware, and a cup of coffee for Garret that he hadn't asked for.

"You're a life saver, Agnes." Garret grinned up at her. "The lady will have a diet cola and then we'll need a few more minutes to order."

"Got it." Agnes winked at him and walked away.

That he remembered what she'd ordered to drink the other day had her stomach fluttering. She doubted Brad ever noticed anything she did, and if he did, there was little hope he'd remember her favorite anything. Fiddling with a fork, she shook the thoughts away and lifted her gaze to meet his. "Did you want coffee?"

"Agnes knows if I stop in after school instead of heading straight home that it's been a long day and I need her coffee." He leaned in and lowered his voice. "Don't tell my mother, but Agnes makes the best coffee in town. Probably in the county, and very possibly in the state."

That made her laugh. He seemed to do that to her a lot. Could she bring herself to look at the job board? To turn the car in at the Midland airport and instead of going to Houston, return to Honeysuckle? That could be a true fresh start. If she hated it, at least she'll have given something new—and safe—a try.

"Something wrong?" Garret had been studying her.

In for a penny, in for a pound. He already knew everything about her, what was one more thing. "Your aunt mentioned a board with work opportunities."

"Yes. There's a lot of word-of-mouth in a small town, but the bulletin board helps folks connect faster." His eyes softened. "So, does this mean that maybe you're thinking of looking for a fresh start here? In Honeysuckle?"

She shrugged. "Bizarre, I know."

"Not necessarily. Here no one knows anything about you. Not your past. Not your problems. It would be a truly fresh start. No judgments."

A smile tugged at her lips. "That does hold a certain appeal."

"What did you do in Houston?"

"Despite having a degree in psychology, I worked as a manager for a small family owned insurance business." She couldn't stop her smile from growing wider. Just thinking about the sweet job she had put her in a happy place. As long as she didn't think about how stupidly she threw it all away.

"Managing a business sounds industry agnostic. There's probably more than one business in town that could use a good manager."

Wouldn't that be nice? If a little hopeful. "Of course, I'd have to find a place to live. Are there are a lot of apartments in town?"

His expression grew more serious. "Not really. A few years back they converted an old warehouse into apartments not far from here. My brother Preston had a place there, but it burned down and they haven't rebuilt yet. Though some folks have turned attics into apartments. A few have done like the northeast and turned larger homes into multifamily units, but not a whole lot. Yet."

"That's what I was afraid of."

His gaze drifted off somewhere, his eyes cooling. She could almost see the wheels turning in his mind, but didn't have the foggiest idea what had him thinking so hard.

Nodding softly, as if trying to convince himself of

something, he blew out a soft sigh. "I may have an idea."

If anyone else on the planet had said that to her, she might be grabbing her purse and heading for the nearest exit, but from Garret, the honorable man who had rescued her from herself, what could she lose by hearing him out?

Where to begin? Right about now, Garret wasn't so sure he hadn't lost his mind. Odds were pretty good that if he proposed what he was thinking, Jacqueline would certainly think him certifiable.

Then again, what was he always telling his students: the worst anyone can say is no, but if you don't ask, you'll never know? "I have an idea, but before you say no, hear me out."

One brow rose higher than the other, the look reminding him of his sister Rachel. "Okay, but should I change from a cola to a stiffer drink?"

Chuckling, he wasn't so sure she was wrong. "Hear me out, then decide."

"I'm listening."

"There are a few things about my family, and ranch, that I didn't share the other day." He looked up at her. Her expression blank, but not closed. So far so good. For the next several minutes, only stopping once to give Agnes their dinner order, he explained to her as quietly as he could about his father's passing, about Ray robbing them nearly blind, then stopped when she reached out and touched his hand.

"I'm so sorry." She leaned back and sighed. "Puts a new perspective on quitting a job that I'd only had a few years, and giving up a rented apartment. Even sneaky, lying Brad doesn't seem so bad after all. At least he didn't steal my money."

"Always a silver lining." He wished theirs was a little shinier.

"And yours?" She picked up her burger again. "Is there

a silver lining for your family?"

Here went nothing. "There's a family trust fund. Set up a couple of hundred years ago by Grover Eugene Sweet."

"Perfect." Her concern for him shifted to a smile.

"Not exactly."

Biting into her burger, she kept her gaze on him.

"The trust only pays out when a Sweet marries."

She nodded. "And your brothers recently married, right?"

"Preston and Carson. Yes."

"So the trust paid off?"

"Not exactly. There's a small up front payment, then a monthly stipend, but the big payoff is on the first anniversary."

Still chewing, she nodded again.

"Sarah Sue was our next-door neighbor and she offered to marry Preston for the trust. In name only," he hurriedly added. "Same happened with Carson, only Jess wasn't a neighbor, she was his college sweetheart. Well, not a sweetheart, more of his college crush, but I digress."

"So they're not really married?" Her forehead crumpled with confusion.

"Oh, they're definitely really married. The bank wouldn't pay the trust if they weren't. And the hardest part at first was making my mother believe they were very much in love and that was the hurry to marry."

The lines in her forehead grew deeper. "I think I'm confused."

"Let me back up. When Rachel suggested the whole idea of marrying for the trust money, we all agreed Mom would never let us do that for the money, not even if it saved the ranch. So we agreed she would not know about the arrangement. They had to fool Mom, and pretty much the whole town."

"And it's worked?" She took another bite, her burger almost finished.

"Better than planned. Everyone is head over heels in love with each other."

Swallowing, she grinned. "So all is well that ends well."

"Not exactly."

"Déjà vu," she teased.

He glanced down at his own burger; he hadn't touched it yet, and he wasn't sure he could. His stomach was rolling and not till this second did he realize how much he wanted her to go for the idea. "We need a lot more money, a lot."

She nodded.

"So we're all trying to get married."

Her hands froze, the burger halfway to her mouth. She'd finally figured out where this was going.

"If you agreed to stay for a year and marry me—in name only—you'd have a place to live, free room and board, I'm sure there's a job that you would enjoy, or at least not hate, or you wouldn't have to work at all if you prefer."

Her burger still frozen in space, the only changes were her mouth had dropped slightly open and her eyes had circled a little wider.

"There could be a bonus paid after the year."

No sounds came from her.

"I know it's crazy."

Her mouth snapped closed, she blinked, and her burger lowered to the plate in front of her. "That's the first thing you've said that makes sense."

"You're right. Forget I said anything." He lifted the burger and wondered if he'd heave if he took a bite.

Letting out a sigh, her shoulders lowered, and she leaned back. "If I say no, you're going to find someone else, aren't you?"

"I have to." He threw up his hands. "We'll lose the ranch if we don't come up with a boatload of money and fast."

"In name only?" she repeated.

He almost dropped his burger. Was she actually considering it? "Yes. Absolutely. No hanky-panky."

She laughed and he had no idea why. "You know, anyone else and I'd say you were a bold-faced liar, but considering how we met, I think I believe you."

"It's the truth. All of it." He held up two fingers.

"Scouts honor."

"Were you a scout?"

He laughed. "Eagle."

"Figures you'd say that. It explains a lot."

"If you knew my mom and dad, it would make even more sense. Old fashioned with a capital O and F."

"Hence why you can't tell her you're marrying to save the ranch."

"Bingo."

"Can I think about it?"

"Of course." She was thinking about it. He wanted to whoop or pump his fist, but a simple smile would have to do.

"How much time do I have?"

Good question, and he was pretty sure, *not much* wasn't what she'd want to hear. "I have an idea."

"Another one?" Instead of shock, or surprise, or confusion, she bit back a laugh. The woman had a sense of humor. Good, she was going to need it moving from Houston to a working cattle ranch.

"You have no place to stay, no money to speak of, and need time to consider. What if you come to the ranch—as a guest for the night—and see for yourself what we'd be up against?"

"The ranch?"

He nodded.

"Now?"

"As good a time as any." He tried to look calm, cool and collected while she thought. Silently lifting prayers for what looked to be the best solution to a serious problem.

"All right." She actually smiled. "One night. One visit. And tomorrow, you'll have my answer.

Hot damn. If all went well, tomorrow they'd be one step closer to saving the ranch—or a year of hell. Maybe he *had* lost his mind.

CHAPTER SEVEN

Keeping an eye on Jacqueline's rental car in the rearview mirror, Garret pulled up the long drive to the ranch house. Parking in front, he hopped out of his truck and hurried around, waiting for Jacqueline to stop and unlock the door. Holding the driver side door open for her, Garret focused on her face, the reaction to the two-story home making him smile.

"So this is what a Texas ranch looks like?"

"Ours at least. Home sweet home." He tried to see it through the eyes of a city person—the barn, the paddock where Blaze and the other horses grazed, the vast expanse of Texas dirt. "Not like Houston."

"No." Her gaze scanned from left to right. "It's beautiful." The wonder in her voice was genuine, and something in Garret's chest loosened.

"I probably should have asked sooner. You're not allergic to dogs, are you?"

Her gaze still taking in the massive home, she shook her head.

"Do you like them? Because we have two."

Again she silently shook her head before dragging her gaze away from the house. "I love dogs. Not a smart thing to have in a big city, but I love them."

He hoped she meant real dogs and not those little nippy things that women kept in their handbags. Before Garret could ask, the front door swung open and Mason bounded out, Brady at his heels.

"Uncle Garret!" Mason called, racing toward the truck. "Dad said you went to town and—" He skidded to a halt when he spotted Jackie. "Who's she?"

"Is that any way to address a lady?"

The boy toed the dirt and shook his head. "Sorry, ma'am. Nice to meet you."

She leaned over, smiling, and extended her hand. "My name is Jackie, what's yours?"

Jackie? He needed to remember to call her by the nickname for Jacqueline.

His nephew brightened. "Mason."

"And who is your friend?" Down on her heels, she turned her hand palm up under Brady's muzzle, scratching behind his ears when the dog dipped his head into her palm. Apparently, Brady approved of Garret's choice for a wife. Temporary wife.

"This is Brady." Mason grinned proudly.

"He's a sweet boy," she said softly.

Mason giggled under his breath. The kid was smart. He caught the unintentional pun.

It took Jackie a moment, but in the middle of scratching the dog, her fingers stilled and she rolled her eyes heavenward, realizing she'd called the Sweet family dog, sweet.

"You three planning on having dinner in the front yard?" Carson called from the front doorway, his smile softening the harshness of his words.

Garret guided Jackie toward the house with a light touch to her elbow. She crossed into the house first, and as Garret passed his brother, Carson raised a questioning brow at him. Explanations would have to wait.

Inside, the house buzzed with activity. Delicious aromas wafted from the kitchen, and Garret could hear his sisters' voices mixed with his mother's laughter. Jackie hesitated at the threshold, and he gave her what he hoped was a reassuring nod.

"Heads up. We've got company," Carson announced as they entered the living room. "Everyone pretend you weren't raised in a barn."

"Carson," his mother's voice carried crisply from the kitchen.

Chuckling, Carson walked over to his mother and

kissed her temple "Sorry, I've always wanted to say that."

Their mom rolled her eyes and shook her head, staring up at the ceiling, a smile on her face. "Where did we go wrong, Charlie? Where?"

Everyone cracked up. They'd finally reached a point in time where the mere mention of their father didn't weigh on them like a lead blanket.

His mother emerged from the kitchen, wiping her hands on a dish towel. Sarah and Jess, his brothers' wives, paused their conversation. Rachel and Jillian appeared from the hallway, their expressions shifting from surprise to barely concealed delight when they spotted Jackie.

"Well, hello there," his mother said, crossing the room with outstretched hands. "I'm Alice Sweet."

"Mom," Garret injected, "this is a friend of mine from Houston. Jackie Drake."

"Thank you for having me, Mrs. Sweet. I hope it's not an imposition."

"Company is always a treasure and never an imposition." His mother beamed at her, then shot Garret a look that clearly said *you should have called ahead*. "You'll stay for dinner, of course."

"Actually." Garret cleared his throat. "I was hoping Jackie could stay the night. It's a long drive to Midland for her flight home and…"

"That road at night is no place for a woman alone. Of course she can stay." His mom finished his thought for him before turning to Jackie. "I'm afraid I confiscated the guest room for a hobby room. You don't mind sharing with a sewing machine, do you?"

The lighthearted comment brought a genuine smile to Jackie's lips. Her whole face lit up. "I'm quite fond of sewing machines, as long as they don't snore."

His mom cackled with delight. "Atta girl"

Rachel and Jillian exchanged a look that made Garret want to groan. His sisters had the subtlety of a pair of bulldozers.

Rachel stepped forward, linking her arm through Jackie's. "Come on, I'll give you the grand tour."

"And I'll help," Jillian added, flanking Jackie's other side.

Garret had an irresistible urge to shout 'stop' and pull Jackie back before his sisters mucked everything up. Then again, how much worse could it be? He was trying to strike a bargain with a near stranger for the most intimate job on the planet—that is, if it were for real.

"She seems nice," Carson said quietly, clapping Garret on the shoulder. Then, lowering his voice, "The internet?"

He shook his head.

Carson stared down the hall his sisters had gone with the new woman in his life. "Interesting timing, an old friend showing up now."

"She's not that old a friend. We met recently in Millers Creek."

"I see." Carson studied his brother.

"She knows about our dilemma. She's, uh, thinking about it."

"Is that a good thing?" Carson was still studying his younger brother.

He shrugged. "I don't know, but I think so."

The entire Sweet family radiated warmth, from Alice's immediate welcome to Mason's boyish curiosity. Even Brady, the dog, had given her his approval, and Jackie couldn't help but feel that was somehow significant. Then why, as Rachel and Jillian led her up the stairs, was her stomach doing back flips.

"So you're from Houston?" Rachel asked, guiding her down a hallway lined with family photos.

"Born in Tyler, but I've been in Houston for the last several years." Jackie paused to look at a portrait of what must have been the whole family, including a man with Garret's eyes who had to be their father. She guessed the Charlie his mother jokingly spoke to about their son.

"What brings you to our little corner of nowhere?"

Jillian asked.

She shrugged. "Thought it was time for a change, but Millers Creek didn't turn out to be the gem I'd hoped for."

The sisters exchanged a sideways glance that had her wondering just how much they knew about how she and Garret met.

"Houston can be a bit much." Jillian waved a hand in the air. "All that traffic and concrete."

"Here we are." Rachel pushed open a door to reveal a cozy room with pale blue walls. A sewing machine sat in one corner near the window, alongside neatly stacked fabric. The double bed looked freshly made, with a patchwork quilt in blues and creams. She wondered if it was homemade. From what she'd seen of the town, it wouldn't surprise her if the whole thing had been hand stitched.

"Mom's been quilting since Dad died," Rachel explained, catching Jackie's glance at the bedspread. "Says it helps her think."

"It's beautiful." Jackie ran her hand over the intricate stitching.

"Bathroom's across the hall." Jillian opened the closet. "Plenty of room." Garret's sister's eyes suddenly held a sparkle they hadn't had a few minutes ago. "You know, in case you decide to stay longer."

Rachel cleared her throat and stared daggers at her sister. "We're just down the hall if you need anything."

Jackie nodded, setting her purse on the bed. She'd have to get her bag out of her car later.

"So," Rachel came by her and sat on the edge of the bed, "how long have you known our brother?"

"Not long," Jackie admitted. "We met in Millers Creek."

Rachel's eyes sparkled with curiosity. "At the Bronco Lounge?"

"Uh…" Heat rushed to Jackie's face. Did it count as having met if she didn't remember? "Sort of."

"Sort of?" Now Jillian looked confused.

A knock at the door interrupted them. Garret stood in the doorway, his expression wary as he took in the three of them. "Everything okay in here?"

"Just girl talk," Jillian answered innocently.

"Dinner's ready." His gaze settled with hers and she wondered would he have told his sisters about her? About his night in a hotel waiting for her to sober up? As all the thoughts ran through her mind, she noticed him very slightly shake his head at her. Had he understood her worries? When his lips curled up in a sweet smile, she realized he'd done just that. He was still taking care of her, even though she'd more than sobered up.

"We'd better get going or Mom will send Brady after us." Rachel sprang up from the bed, following her sister out the door.

Garret remained in the doorway, waiting for her. "They're right. Mom's a stickler about being on time for dinner."

Downstairs, the dining room table was full except for two chairs, one for her and one for Garret. There was no awkwardness, no lags in conversations; the siblings teased each other and laughed with each other, and their mother, and once or twice, included her on the joke. It was as if she'd always been a part of the family. With every passing minute, she felt more and more at ease in this big old house that had sheltered generations of his family. Jackie felt a pang of longing for what Garret and his family represented—roots, connection, belonging. Not that she didn't love her grandmother, but it had just been the three of them for so many years, and once she moved to Houston, except for Grams, Tyler didn't really feel like home. Not like this.

In the kitchen after dinner, she had to insist, but was allowed to help clear the table and now the kitchen.

"I know most people like to use the dishwasher, and with this bunch I'd be nuts not to, but I prefer to wash my grandmother's platters by hand." Alice Sweet handed her a wet platter to dry. "He's a good man."

It took her a moment to make the connection between the platters and the good man, mostly when she realized one had nothing to do with the other, and she was pretty sure the good man was Garret. "He's definitely a gentleman."

Alice didn't look at her, but she continued to scrub one platter in particular, finally speaking without looking up. "If you think you'd like to visit a bit longer, you're welcome to stay as long as you like." Then her head turned to face Jackie. "I mean that. My children's friends are always welcome."

"Thank you." She nodded. "Honeysuckle seems to be more than I expected. I'll think about it."

Alice smiled. "You do that."

Garret came into the kitchen from outside. "Samson is all set for the night."

"With Brady's help, that dog has come a long way." Alice tugged the towel from Jackie's hands and faced her son. "Why don't you show our guest around outside? There aren't any evening skies like this in Houston."

Jackie hesitated a moment, but Alice nudged her out of the way.

When the back door closed behind them, Garret smiled at her. "One thing folks learn fast around here, is there's no point in arguing with my mother."

"I'll remember that." She tore her gaze away from Garret. The man was many things and handsome was at the top of the list. Those blue eyes could win over a dozen women in a heartbeat. So, where did all this leave her? And how would her life turn out if she agreed to this crazy scheme to save this amazing ranch and—no pun intended—sweet family? She supposed there would be only one way to find out. Spinning about, she met Garret's gaze. "I'll do it."

CHAPTER EIGHT

Last night they'd had little chance to talk about the plans for their temporary marriage. Within a few minutes of Jackie informing him she was willing to partake in the next charade, one by one and two by two, his siblings, and his mom, had joined them on the back porch. They'd all laughed and joked and teased, and it had done Garret's heart good to see Jackie laughing along with everyone. The one thing they had managed to discuss was the need to return the rental car to the Midland airport.

So, first thing this morning, he'd called the school to tell them to get a substitute for the day and he'd followed her on the hours' long drive. Now, Garret watched the rental car lot shrink in the rearview mirror.

Seated beside him on the passenger seat, Jackie watched the traffic ahead, her hands loosely resting on her lap, her shoulders remained stiff, her gaze fixed on the entrance ramp that would bring them back to Honeysuckle. No doubt, now that the first step to moving to Honeysuckle was out of the way, she was thinking the same thing he was; what the hell were they going to do next?

"So, are you hungry?" He glanced over at her.

"Not really." Jackie met his gaze. "If I keep eating your mother's breakfasts while living out here, I'm going to be as big as that house of yours."

Even when she was nervous, she could make him laugh. "I doubt that."

"I don't." Her focus returned to gazing out the window at the vast, flat Texas landscape blurring past them. "Is everything out here this flat and empty? Most of the way here, I barely saw anything in the distance."

"There was a cow."

She flung around in her seat. "You saw it? The one lonesome cow?"

"With nothing else around it." He smiled. "Oh, yeah."

"Shouldn't there have been a barn, or a house, or other cows, or something?"

He chuckled again. "Maybe, but that one probably broke a fence line somewhere. His people will find him sooner than later."

"Wow." She twisted back to face forward, her shoulders a tad more relaxed.

"This would be a good time to discuss exactly what you've gotten yourself into." Without hesitation, he stretched out his arm and took hold of her hand. She jumped slightly at the unexpected gesture. "This is the first thing that you'll have to get used to. If we're supposed to be in love, and soon happily married, we're going to have to hold hands, hug, and," he tried not to choke on the words, "kiss—sometimes—even in public."

She nodded, but kept her hand in his.

Her profile was calm, thoughtful, but he couldn't quite gauge what was going on behind those green eyes. "What are you thinking?"

"That I might be crazy."

He let go of her hand.

Instantly, without hesitation, she snatched it back. "On the other hand, sanity is highly overrated."

"Fair enough." So much had to be broached.

"I'll want to work. I know I'm helping your family out, but I still want to earn my keep."

"You're doing more than helping. You're saving us."

"God has a sense of humor."

"How is that?"

"I can't even save myself, and yet here I am, helping save a two-hundred-year-old ranch."

"You understand that we have to convince my mother, and quickly, that we're in love and don't want to wait to marry?"

She nodded.

"So far, my brothers have avoided a church wedding, but Mom's itching for a big shindig. If she insists on a church wedding, will that be a deal breaker?"

Those shoulders stiffened again. "I don't suppose *I don't know* is the answer you wanted."

"If it's honest, yes, that's the answer I want."

She turned to face him again. "Honest?"

He nodded.

"I'm scared to death, but I'm more scared of what will happen to me if I don't stay."

"I'm not sure that's the response to a proposal that a normal man would want to hear, but I promise you this, no matter what, I will never lie to you."

"Okay." She bobbed her head, still holding his hand. "Ditto."

"There won't be any money in this for you until after the year. By then we should be able to give you a little bundle for you to set yourself up where you want, but I'd be lying if I were to tell you it will be a lot."

"I understand. Seems fair enough. After all, I'll be getting free room and board. I've been paying rent since I went off to college. That alone will be a tidy savings."

"Yes, well, about that room and board. As I mentioned yesterday, the only real apartment building in town burned down a while back. It's where Preston used to live. Anyhow, there's a good chance that we're going to have to stay at the ranch."

"Okay."

"Which means, we'll have to share a room."

Her lips pressed together tightly, and her eyes bore into him.

"It will still be in name only," he reassured. "Strictly business."

"Business," she muttered.

He had a feeling he was going to be reminding himself of that a whole heck of a lot over the next year or so. Especially since right about now, all he could think about was how the sunlight caught the gold strands in her blonde hair, how her hand rested so lightly in his, and how dang right it all felt.

Right or not, if he didn't let go of her hand, he might do or say something really stupid. Just about then, he spotted the road sign flashing past: Monahans Sandhills State Park – Next Exit. An idea, impulsive and utterly ridiculous, sparked in his brain. He'd been so focused on the practicalities, the business, he'd forgotten none of that meant there couldn't be… fun.

"How do you feel about sand?"

"Excuse me?" Surely in the middle of discussing sleeping arrangements for their temporary marriage, he'd not asked about sand? Then again, the last two days had been a little bit like *Alice in Wonderland*. For all she knew, she'd fallen down a rabbit hole.

"Ever seen a sand dune?"

Yep. He'd said sand. "Do the bumps by the beach at Galveston count?"

"Nope." His mouth widened in a grin that almost took over his face. "Hang on, you're about to see your first, honest-to-goodness, sand dune."

"Sand dunes," Jackie breathed, as the truck drove under the massive arch at the entrance to the state park.

Garret pulled into a parking spot in front of a single level building. Inside, he paid the entrance fee and took her over to the area that carried round discs in every color imaginable. He turned to her, a hint of a smile playing on his lips. "Ready to try something completely ridiculous?"

As if leaving Houston, showing up at Brad's door, and now moving clear across the state to a small town almost impossible to find on a map, and marrying a man she barely knew wasn't ridiculous enough. Lately her life had become a master class in the absurd. Ridiculous had become her new normal. "Sure."

From where she stood, she watched as Garret slung the discs over his shoulder, the bright green and red plastic circles a stark contrast to his pale blue chambray shirt. When he turned back to her, his eyes were warm with amusement, and something else… something that made her breath catch in her throat.

"Let's go." His hand at the small of her back, he nudged her forward.

Together, they trudged up the slope. With every step, her feet sank deep in the sand. Finally, at the top of the first dune, she was pretty sure her jaw had just dropped wide open. Hills—no, more like mountains of pale golden sand rose against the bright blue sky. She could only imagine that this must be what the Sahara Desert looked like. Her gaze shifted to the bottom of the steep slope. "Uh, I don't know about this."

"Don't tell me Jacqueline Drake is afraid of a little sand," Garret teased, holding out the bright red disc to her.

"It's not the sand I'm worried about." Shaking her head, she cautiously took hold of the disc. "It's the stopping part."

"That's the beauty of it." He set the green disc down on the edge of the dune. "You don't have to worry about stopping—the sand does it for you. It's easy. Watch."

He sat down on the disc, legs extended in front of him, and pushed off with both hands. Zooming down the dune, kicking up a spray of sand behind him, his whoop of delight echoed back to her. About three quarters of the way down, the disc slowed naturally, coming to a gentle stop at the bottom. He stood up, sand clinging to his jeans, arms raised in triumph. "See? Easy!" he called up to her.

Jackie clutched the red disc. "You're out of your mind!"

"Probably!" he shouted back, grinning. "Come on, city girl. Live a little!"

Taking a deep breath, she placed the disc at the edge just as he had done. This was ridiculous. She was a grown woman about to slide down a mountain of sand on a plastic disc. She'd been spontaneous and daring following after Brad, and look where that got her. Crazy wasn't all it was cracked up to be, and yet, looking at Garret's expectant face below, it struck her, with the right man, some chances were worth taking. She flashed a wide smile to accompany her teasing tone. "If I break something, you're driving me to the hospital!"

"Deal!"

Lowering herself onto the disc, she extended her legs the way Garret had done. Teetering at the edge, her heart hammered rapidly in her chest. Before she could reconsider, she pushed off with both hands.

The initial drop made her stomach lurch, and a startled shriek escaped her lips, followed by sheer exhilaration. The disc picked up speed, and the wind whipped her hair about. Sand sprayed up on either side, tickling her arms and face. Without meaning to, she let out a laugh that built into a full-throated whoop of joy. The disc gradually slowed on its own, coming to rest just a few feet from where Garret stood, applauding wildly.

"That was amazing!" she gasped, her heart still racing frantically.

"You're a natural." He offered his hand to help her up, pulling her to her feet with such enthusiasm that she stumbled forward, colliding with his chest. His hands steadied her shoulders, and for a moment, they stood too close, sand-dusted and breathless.

"Sorry," she murmured, stepping back.

"Don't be," he replied softly, then cleared his throat. "Ready to go again?"

Twenty minutes later, they'd climbed the dune three more times, racing each other down on parallel paths. Jackie's sides ached from laughing, and sand had worked its way into every possible crevice of her clothing. She collapsed at the bottom of the dune after their fourth run, flopping back to make a sand angel.

"I can't believe I've lived in Texas my whole life and never done this."

Garret dropped down beside her, still clutching his disc. "It's one of those hidden treasures. Dad used to bring us here when we were kids. Mom would pack a picnic, and we'd spend the whole day sliding down, climbing up, sliding down again."

The wistful note in his voice made her turn her head to

look at him. Sand clung to his dark hair, and a smudge marked his cheek. Without thinking, she reached out and brushed it away. His eyes met hers, curious and warm. "You miss him," she said simply.

Garret nodded. "Every day. But being here—it brings back the good stuff. Makes him feel closer somehow."

"Thank you for bringing me," Jackie let her hand fall back to the sand. "For sharing this with me."

A slow smile spread across his face. "Well, if you're going to be my temporary wife, you might as well know what you're getting into. The Sweet family tradition of completely ridiculous fun."

"Is that written into the contract? Mandatory ridiculous fun?"

"It's non-negotiable," he said gravely, then broke into a grin. "Along with getting sand absolutely everywhere."

"I think I can live with those terms," she laughed, sitting up and shaking sand from her hair.

Garret stood up and offered his hand again. "One more run?"

Looking up at him—this man she barely knew and yet was about to sort of marry—Jackie felt something shift inside her. Maybe it was the childlike joy of sliding down sand dunes, or maybe it was the way he'd shared something personal, a memory of his father. Whatever it was, for the first time since arriving in West Texas, the idea of staying didn't feel quite so crazy.

She took his hand, letting him pull her to her feet. "Race you to the top!"

CHAPTER NINE

The door to their father's study closed with a soft click as Jillian, the last to arrive, slipped inside. This had become the go-to-meeting place whenever they had something serious to discuss—or plan. Garret glanced around at his siblings; Carson seated at their father's desk, Rachel curled up in the worn leather chair by the window, Preston standing with arms crossed near the bookcase. The familiar scent of leather, old books, and maybe even their dad's cologne, lingered in the air.

"So," Rachel broke the silence, "how did the drive go?"

"Things are coming together. I'm hopeful we'll work it all out."

Jillian plopped down on the nearby chair. "Well, Mom clearly likes her."

"Definitely," Carson agreed. "She seemed thrilled when y'all told her at dinner that she'd be staying a bit longer."

"Yeah," Rachel said. "It was a good strategy to pretend how long hinged on whether or not she found a job."

Waving a single arm in the air, Jillian sighed. "Well, it's not like they could tell her she's staying for a year to pretend marry Garret and collect on the trust."

"Is she really looking for work?" Carson swirled the cubes in his drink.

Garret nodded. "Yes, we stopped at the café. She pulled two opportunities from the bulletin board."

"Which ones?" Rachel shifted in her seat.

"Town clerk assistant and an admin position at the high school."

"Remind me what she did in Houston?" Preston asked.

"Operations manager for a small insurance company."

"That's right." Preston's head bobbed.

"So she's really staying?" Jillian leaned forward, elbows on her knees.

Garret nodded, feeling a strange mix of relief and something else he couldn't quite name. "We hammered out most of the details on the drive back."

"So when's the big announcement?" Rachel grinned, a mischievous glint in her eye. "And the wedding?"

"There's the challenge. We couldn't figure out a way to move things along quickly without drawing suspicion from Mom. After all, I can't exactly blurt out over breakfast, *Isn't Jackie great? We're getting married next week.*"

"That might be a bit odd." Preston shrugged.

"What if," Carson leaned forward on the desk, "you don't make it seem sudden? Say you've been talking online for months. Finally, met in person in Millers Creek, which is true enough."

"And it was love at first sight," Jillian added with dramatic flair, hands clasped to her heart.

"Less is more," Carson advised. "Don't over explain. Just say you reconnected, things clicked, and you both realized no point in wasting time when you find the right person."

"Worked for me," Preston said with a smile.

"And me," Carson agreed.

"Speaking of clicking," Rachel's gaze sharpened on Garret, "how's that going? You two seemed pretty cozy at dinner."

Garret felt heat creep up his neck. "We get along well. It's… easy being around her."

"Good, because this needs to move along sooner than later." Carson leaned back in his seat again. "You'll need to start cozying up in front of Mom."

"And the town," Rachel added. "Don't forget the town."

"And you'd better get your stories straight, because Mom will eventually get around to the questions of how you met, how long have you known each other, etc." Jillian shrugged at her brother. "Otherwise, things could get complicated."

As if marrying a near stranger wasn't complicated enough. "I can handle complicated," Garret said.

"Good," Preston said. "Because you're about to get a whole lot of it."

"Okay," Jillian stood, "let's be practical. We've had two quick marriages in a row. If we don't want Mom to get suspicious, we have to come up with an exact plan."

Garret nodded, it was why they'd all come together, a good idea or two was what he'd hoped for. "Have something specific in mind?"

"Of course I do. Think of this as any other courtship. Sit down with Mom, talk to her. Tell her how much you like Jackie. How there's something about her that is different and special."

That would be easy enough, so far Jillian hadn't said anything that wasn't true. He'd known from the moment Jackie put on a good face and slid down the sand hill even though he could see how scared she was that she wasn't like any other woman he'd known. Simply having agreed to this hare-brained trust scheme, reinforced how special she was, and he really did think about her more than he should.

Rachel frowned at her sister. "You *want* him to tell Mom what he's planning?"

"Hear me out." Jillian stared daggers at her twin. "Ask Mom what she thinks of Jackie. We all know Mom is a romantic at heart, and she seems to really like Jackie, so she'll have some profound bit of wisdom for you. Then ask her, is it crazy to court her? Of course Mom will look at you like you have nine heads because no one courts a girl anymore, but if you play it right, I think she'll not only buy it, I bet she'll help you win over the girl of your dreams."

Girl of his dreams. Is that what Jackie was? No, he shook his head. This is pretend. But courting?

"You know," Rachel piped up, "she has a point. Lay your intentions on the table and get Mom's help. Then the proposal won't be a surprise."

"In the meantime," Preston added, "take her out, show her off, and let the gossip start. It'll take a little acting, but if Jackie is in agreement, I think Jillian's idea is a good one."

"Of course it's a good one." Jillian made a silly face at her brother before patting herself on the shoulder. "I'm brilliant."

"Ha," Rachel scoffed. "Don't pat yourself on the back too hard, you might fall off that pedestal."

Most of the room broke out in short chuckles or muffled laughter. But the important thing was they all agreed. And they had a plan.

His siblings filed out of the study, each giving him an encouraging nod or thumbs up as they passed. Garret stayed behind for a moment. His father's presence seemed especially strong tonight, and Garret could almost hear his advice: *Plans are good, son, but life rarely follows them.* For the first time he could remember, he really hoped his father wasn't right.

A rap on her door pulled Jackie away from the most boring book she'd ever picked up. "Come in."

"I'm not disturbing you, am I?"

She shook her head. "No, I thought I'd relax a little before tackling the two applications."

"Need some help?" Garret remained in the doorway, his feet planted firmly in the hall, his head peeking inside.

"Couldn't hurt." Closing the book and setting it on the nightstand, she reached for the papers beside her, and crossing her legs, patted the foot of the bed for Garret to take a seat.

The way he walked slowly toward her bed, anyone would think he was facing a firing squad, not an application for her employment.

"I think I'd like to apply for the school job first."

His head bobbed as he slowly descended onto the edge of the bed. Any more on the edge and he'd be sitting on the floor. "Any reason in particular?"

"I've worked in a stressful industry; I can't help but think working for the city could be equally stressful. A school, on the other hand, shouldn't be high maintenance, and," she sprouted a grin, "summer vacations!"

Chuckling, Garret looked at the application for the high school office position. "I can't argue. Summers off is quite the perk."

"Is that the voice of experience talking?" One of the many things she appreciated about spending time with Garret was the ease with which conversation came. For the most part, after only a few days, she felt like there wasn't anything they couldn't discuss, or share.

"I've had a nice vacation or two. On a teacher's budget, of course." His smile widened and he shifted a little further onto the bed.

She liked that he was becoming more comfortable around her. "Of course."

Frowning, Garret carefully eyed the paper in his hand. "I'm surprised they're not asking you to attach a resume."

"They're not?" She scooted forward, shifting to kneeling like a curious puppy looking at the paper in his master's hand, hoping it was a snack.

"Look for yourself." He handed her the paper and she sat back on her rear. "Well, that is odd." Her gaze lifted, meeting his. "Do you think I should attach one anyway? If you have a printer here, I can access it from the cloud storage and then print it."

"We do. And I suppose it wouldn't hurt."

Reaching for a pen, she began filling out the obvious, her name, birth date, and then paused. "Is it going to look weird if I use the address here?"

He shook his head. "Not after I start courting you."

Pen in hand, her head snapped up. "Excuse me?"

"You say that a lot, don't you?" He smiled.

"My grandmother would have my head if I said *what*. That drove her nuts. Especially when she called my name. I learned to respond with *coming!*"

"Got it. Anyhow, we decided to try a different approach this time. I'm going to ask Mom's advice on courting you."

"Courting?

He nodded.

"Like in the nineteenth century?"

"I suppose. Or that TV show with that religious family and a bazillion kids. I think Mom will really buy into the old-fashioned charm."

"If you say so."

"What we do need to work out is the story I'm going to tell her about how we met. I was thinking… Last summer I took our class on an outing to NASA. Can you think of any way we could have run into each other?"

That took a little thought. "NASA isn't exactly in the middle of downtown Houston or near where I live. Of course, your mother doesn't have to know where I live." She thought a little more and then leaned forward again. "Where did y'all have lunch?"

"Lunch?" He looked to the ceiling a moment "Some lunch joint. Nothing special."

"Rudy's is a favorite barbecue place. They're all over Texas but more in Houston and Austin. We could say we met there during lunch. I had to wait for all the kids to order and you were very kind and stopped the next kid from ordering so I could get my order in first."

"Well, that was nice of me." That smile was doing weird things to her stomach. "And I actually do love Rudy's. Their creamed corn is to die for."

"Right?" She sat up, absurdly excited to learn he liked the same food she did. As good as their barbecue was, it was the corn that kept her coming in to eat.

"But we didn't see each other again until you had a job opportunity in Millers Creek—that, of course, didn't pan out?"

She wasn't quite sure if that was a statement or a question, so she simply nodded.

"Good, then we have a plan?"

"We do." It felt oddly nice to be working together with Garret.

He pushed to his feet, and extended his hand to her. "Come on. I'll take you downstairs to Dad's study and you can print that resume for the application."

Immediately her fingers curled around his and her

stomach did that funny rolling thing again. She'd expected him to let go of her hand once she was standing, but he didn't. He held on as they left the room, walked down the hall, descended the stairs, and then crossed into the study. What she didn't know, was if this had been simply for show, hoping to bump into his mother, or if this was real. In her head she understood this was probably just the first of many performances for family and friends, but still a small part of her kind of hoped maybe it was just a little real.

CHAPTER TEN

A day of hunching over student papers had Garret's shoulders aching deep in his bones. Seventh graders weren't exactly known for their penmanship, and after reading thirty essays on the Civil War, his eyes burned almost as much as his back. A hot shower and maybe ten minutes of quiet before dinner would do the trick.

The house was unusually quiet. Dropping his satchel by the door, he called out, "Mom?"

"In here," his mother's voice carried from the kitchen. She was elbow deep in bread dough. "How was school?"

"The usual." He glanced around the kitchen. "Where's Jackie?"

"Out in the barn with Clint."

"Clint?" Something uncomfortable settled in Garret's chest.

"He's showing her how to muck stalls." Eyes twinkling with amusement, his mother straightened, her gaze locking with his. "Clint was in here giving me an update on the wild horses' movements, and how the fence lines have been holding up. When he said he'd be off to muck the stalls, she offered to help."

"She did?" That should have surprised him, and yet, somehow, it didn't.

"I asked her if she knew what it meant, and had she ever done it." His mom chuckled. "I'll tell you something. For a city girl, she's got gumption."

Considering she was willing to take him on for a year, all to save a stranger's family ranch, gumption might be the perfect word to describe Jacqueline Drake. Kissing his mom on the cheek, he crossed the yard, making his way to the barn. He could hear laughter before he even reached the wide doors—Jackie's bright giggle followed by Clint's deeper chuckle. The sound made something twist in his gut.

Pulling open the door, he squinted into the dimmer interior. Jackie stood in the center aisle, a pitchfork in hand, her hair pulled back in a messy ponytail. Wisps had escaped to frame her face. It was a nice face.

Clint leaned against a stall door, one elbow resting on, or perhaps balancing, his own pitch fork. Objectively, Garret knew Clint was good-looking in that weathered cowboy way. The lone ranch hand probably looked much younger than his actual years. For a second Garret contemplated a number, settling on late forties, give or take half a dozen. Much older than Jackie, but not that much older. It shouldn't have bothered him, except, it did.

"How's it going?" Garret stepped into the barn.

"Garret! I didn't hear you come in." A smile firmly intact, she gestured proudly to a half-cleaned stall. "I'm learning to muck."

"So I see." He couldn't help returning her smile, the knot in his chest loosening at her obvious delight.

Clint straightened, then glanced at his watch. "Think I've got enough daylight left to check some more fence line." He tipped his hat to Jackie. "You're doing fine work, Miss Jackie. Garret can show you how to lay down fresh bedding."

"Thanks for the lesson," Jackie called to the ranch hand's retreating back.

As soon as Clint was gone, Garret moved closer, taking in the sight of Jackie in dusty jeans and one of his sister's old flannel shirts, sleeves rolled up to her elbows. "So, mucking stalls, huh?"

"Don't laugh." She teasingly pointed the pitchfork at him. "It's harder than it looks."

"I'm not laughing." Though he couldn't quite suppress his smile. "I'm impressed. Most people's idea of getting to know ranch life involves horses and sunsets, not horse manure."

"Go big or go home," she quipped, then wrinkled her

nose. "Though I'll admit, the smell takes some getting used to."

"You never really get used to it." Garret reached for the pitchfork Clint had hung on the wall. "But you do stop noticing after a while."

They worked side by side, finishing the stall she'd started. Garret showed her how to spread fresh straw, explaining why some parts needed more bedding than others. The work was familiar and oddly companionable, their conversation flowing easily between them. Why was it that hard work could seem like fun with a woman at your side? No, not any woman. Jackie.

"So how was school today?" Her back to him, Jackie spread straw in the corner.

"Long. Parent-teacher conferences are coming up, so everyone's on edge." He gathered another armful of straw. "Tommy Fisher tried to argue that the Confederacy secretly won the Civil War."

"Bold strategy," she laughed. "What'd you tell him?"

"That his secret historical knowledge would be more convincing if he could spell Confederacy correctly."

She had to admit, this guy's easy-going manner, and casual sense of humor, could make any day brighter. Heaven knew, he'd certainly managed to turn her world around.

Surveying their finished work, she promptly declared, "Perfect." Honestly, she couldn't remember being more proud of an accomplishment in her life. Brushing straw from her hands, she turned and caught Garret watching her. "What? Do I have something on my face?"

"Just a little..." Garret reached out, brushing a piece of straw from her cheek. His fingers lingered a moment too long, and yet, not long enough.

"Thanks," she murmured.

A twinkle appeared in his eyes. He flashed her a look

that had her taking a step back. Keeping an eye on him, she watched a smile tilt north to match the sparkle in his eyes as he slowly reached down and grabbing fistfuls of loose straw, took a single step closer and dropped every strand on her head.

"Hey!" she gasped, straw raining down around her face.

"Just helping you get the full ranch experience," his words coming through a muffled laugh.

"Oh?" Setting the pitch fork aside, she shoved her sleeves a little higher. "Game on, cowboy." She scooped up her own handful and flung it at him, hitting him square in the chest.

What followed was nothing short of warfare—straw flying in all directions, laughter bouncing off the barn walls as they chased each other around the stalls. Jackie ducked behind a support beam, and Garret feinted left before circling right, catching her by surprise. She squealed as he dumped another handful of straw over her head, then stumbled backward, losing her balance. His arm shot out, catching her around the waist, pulling her against him to keep her from falling.

Suddenly they were very close, both breathing hard, bits of straw clinging to their clothes and hair. Her hands resting against his chest where she'd braced herself, she was suddenly all too aware of his arm still around her waist, and the strength of the muscled wall under her fingertips.

"Hi." Her voice came out so softly, she wasn't sure she'd actually heard it. Dang, did this man have gorgeous eyes.

"Hi." The single word came out rough and gravely, and for a long moment, neither of them moved.

A horse whinnied from a nearby stall, and whatever spell had them frozen in each other's space, broke.

Quickly, she stepped back, brushing straw from her shirt, praying her face didn't betray the heat she felt flushing her cheeks. Feeling surprisingly awkward, she vaguely waved in the direction of the house. "I should, um, probably clean up before dinner."

"Yeah, me too." He ran a hand through his hair to

dislodge several pieces of straw. "Mom will have a fit if we track all this into the house."

She was oddly overcome with an urge to reach out and help him. To run her fingers through that thick dark hair. Suddenly, visions of soon sharing a room with him flickered in her mind. What she needed was more distance between them and took another large step in retreat.

They walked back together, a new awareness humming between them. Just before they reached the porch, Jackie glanced at him, amusement teasing her lips. "For the record," her smile widened, "I'm pretty sure I won that round."

"Only because I let you." Garret laughed. The tension dissipating, he took hold of her hand and squeezed it tightly. "Time to get this show on the road."

And wasn't that just a darn shame.

The moment the two of them crossed the threshold into the kitchen, the hum of chatting voices slowed. Making sure his mother had seen their clasped hands, Garret regretfully let go of his link with Jackie and followed her inside. What he hadn't expected was the sudden bustle of activity as first Jillian slung a dish rag over the back of a chair and announced, "I have some ideas for new candle scents. I think I'm going to head to my room and work on it before supper." Then Rachel followed with, "I've got some files I need to update," quickly disappearing to her room. Next thing he knew, Carson and Jess were dragging Jackie into the living room to watch some special on PBS that couldn't be missed.

He was pretty sure neither his brother nor the man's wife could have cared less about PBS, but here he was, alone with his mother in the kitchen. Recognizing what the family had done, no time like the present to start the tumbleweed blowing on the upcoming marriage charade.

Her breadmaking done, and the loaves in the oven

filling the house with delicious aromas that would make any man drool, Alice Sweet was now peeling potatoes.

"Can I help?"

She cocked her head and closed one eye while staring at him, then shrugged. "Never can have too much help in the kitchen."

Standing at her side, he began working on the first potato, the peels falling onto the newspaper covered counter. "I've been thinking."

His mom continued to peel the potatoes without looking at him.

"Did Dad court you?"

Her hand froze, and then a slow smile bloomed. "Some might call it that."

"Why?"

She returned to peeling. "According to your father, he decided he wanted to marry me the first time he laid eyes on me. But he had the good sense to realize if he'd proposed that same day, I'd have suggested the men in white coats come and take him away."

Garret nodded. Made sense to him. Though right about now, a few people might suggest the men in white coats come take him away for what he was planning. "Dad always told us that when you know you know, but he never said what he did to win you over."

Dropping a peeled potato in a pot of water, his mother reached for another. "Well, the day after we met, he sent me a dozen roses and all he did was sign it, 'with admiration, Charlie'."

"That sounds kind of lame." He hadn't meant to criticize his dad, but surely the guy could have been more creative.

"It was perfect. Anything more and I'd have thought him a player."

"Hmm. Then what?"

"Every day it was a little something more. Somehow he found out that I loved Nora Roberts books and he sent me her latest release. Then another day it was a bouquet of balloons."

"Balloons? Isn't that rather childish?"

His mom's smile brightened like the sun. "It was endearing like your father. By the end of the week when he called to ask me to join him for dinner, I would have joined him on a trip to the moon if he'd asked."

"Really?"

"Really. Of course, y'all know your dad and I only dated for three months before we got married."

It might be a sign of a bad son, but Garret actually had forgotten that part of their parents' romance.

"You, uh, thinking about courting someone?" his mother didn't look up, just kept peeling the potatoes.

"Mm hm."

Her head bobbed. "Wouldn't be Jackie in the other room, would it?"

It was his turn to nod.

With a shrug, his mom turned to face him, waving the peeler in his face. "Follow your heart and you can't go wrong."

This time, his cheeks tugged a smile out of him and potato in one hand and peeler in the other; he flung his arms around her. "Thanks, Mom."

Mission accomplished. He had her blessing to court Jackie. He felt like throwing a fist pump in the air, and then it hit him, none of this was real—and wasn't that just a bloody shame.

CHAPTER ELEVEN

So far, all was well with the world. At least the part where the Sweet siblings all married for a year to save the ranch. Garret's mom was happy as a pig in slop, grinning every time he and Jackie walked into a room, every time she spotted him standing close, intentionally gazing at her as if she had been plucked from heaven just for him, when he brought her flowers, and her favorite candy tied to a balloon that still floated in her room. All in just a couple of days.

Adding to everyone's good mood, Jackie heard from the high school sooner than anyone had expected that she'd gotten the job. The principal was delighted to have someone with Jackie's skills apply for the position. The woman fawned over Jackie as if afraid her new hire would have a thunderbolt revelation that she was too good for a small-town administrative job.

Now came the next challenge. Getting the town's gossip mill on board with the plan.

Gentle fingertips brushed across his shoulder. He knew exactly who stood behind him. "Sleep well?" Jackie glanced casually across the kitchen, noticing his mother's gaze nonchalantly on the two of them, and kissed him on the temple.

Never in his life had he been so intrigued by a mere kiss on the side of his head. A small part of him thought back to that old television show about being lost in space and the robot shouting *Danger Will Robinson, danger*. Deep down, his inner robot knew this whole plan was like a kid playing with matches—someone was going to get burned, and he was pretty sure, when Jackie walked away in a little more than a year, he was going to be the one thoroughly singed.

"I'm ready if you are." Inching back, Jackie's tone held the same sweetness as her smile.

"Corn hole here we come." Standing, he took hold of her hand. After all, he had a part to play.

His mom looked up from the sink. "Oh, you're going to town today?"

"The four of us. Rachel and Jillian are coming too," he supplied.

A few more minutes, some chatter and the four were in the car heading to town.

"We'd be there by now if you'd let me drive," Rachel sighed from the back seat.

"And that," Jillian smiled too sweetly at her twin, "is why Garret's driving."

Crossing her arms, Rachel made a momentary attempt at being insulted before letting her arms fall to her side and leaning forward, beamed at her brother and Jackie. "I say things are going well, don't you think?"

Garret nodded. He didn't really want to have a detailed conversation about how often he'd suddenly found himself wishing at least some of this was for real.

In town, he pulled into an available parking spot close to the park. The three women hopped out, and elbows linked, made themselves at home at the open court closest to the street. They'd planned all of this ahead, of course—well, maybe not the linked elbows. He had a feeling that it was just some female bonding going on. If Jackie were really a lifetime love partner, the way the three were getting along like a house on fire would have been a good thing.

"Okay." Rachel rubbed her hands together with more enthusiasm than the situation called for. "It will be Jill and me against you and Garret."

Jackie nodded and looked at him, her gaze a little lost. The urge to squeeze her hand and reassure her that she was going to be great was stronger than he'd anticipated, and since they were supposed to put on a show for the town, he went ahead and did what came naturally. Not only did he squeeze her hand, he gave her the slightest of pecks on the lips. "You've got this."

As expected, Jillian and Rachel had aced all their tosses. On her first throw, Jackie's bean bag flew across the wooden board and landed almost a foot away. "Oops?"

There was no stopping the chuckle that escaped from deep in his throat at her innocent expression. He was pretty sure she'd done that on purpose to help with the act, but regardless, she looked so darn cute. "Let me show you." Standing behind her, he brushed up close, his breath momentarily catching in his throat before he found the strength to take her right hand in his and slowly swing her arm forward and back again. "It's an easy motion."

"Easy," she repeated.

Doing it once again, this time with a bag in her hand, he led her arm forward and back and then on the forward swing, whispered in her ear, "Let it go."

She dropped it right on the floor beside her.

This time he forced a soft chuckle. She might be acting, but he was pretty sure her reaction to his voice was purely carnal, and that made him happier than it should have. A few more tries and he stood back, letting her toss the bag. A hole in one. While he'd like to think he was a darn good teacher, he had to accept that Jackie was more likely a darn good actress.

After an hour or so of putting on a show for the town, and beating his sisters quite handsomely, they were all set to head to the café for a late lunch when Aunt Vicky appeared.

Hurrying up to them, his aunt was practically out of breath, her grin wide and her gaze settling on Jackie. "I see we have another champion in town."

It took Jackie a moment to realize his aunt was excited about her. Her hand flew to her chest as her head shook feverishly from side to side. "Not me. I'm just learning."

"Well then, if this is beginning, I can't wait to see how you play after a little more practice!"

"We were just heading to lunch." Jillian smiled at her aunt. "Would you like to join us?"

For a second Garret thought his sister might have lost her mind, and then he remembered, they had a town to convince and his aunt Vicky would be as good as Iris Hathaway at spreading the word.

"Thank you, dear." His aunt rested her hand on Jillian's arm. "I wish I could but I need to get back to the shop." She turned to face Garret. "Which is really why I came over. There are a few boxes in the back of my pickup that need to go into the store room and they weigh more than I do. Could you please help us unload them?"

"Of course." He reached for Jackie's hand. "I'll only be a few minutes. Why don't you ladies go ahead and get us a table?"

All three women nodded and he wondered, not for the first time, if he was getting into much more than he could handle for a whole year.

"No, Grams, I'm fine. Really I am. I know. Yes, change can be good." Or tough. Or maybe just a bit of a miracle. "No, I don't need any money." Not any more. "I have a nice place to stay. How much?" She probably shouldn't have told her grandmother she'd left Houston. Avoiding the never-ending questions was becoming harder and harder. "What? No, I'm not being evasive." But now she was fibbing. Sometimes she felt like her grandmother still saw her as the ten-year-old girl, confused by the sudden loss of her mom, and lying to her now, that's exactly how she felt. Nodding at her grandmother's ramblings about staying warm, safe, and eating well, her gaze landed at the far corner of the café. It couldn't be. Could it? Her brows buckled and she narrowed her eyes in an effort to see more clearly. How could that be?

"Is something wrong?" Jillian and Rachel's heads bounced left then right, from her to the direction she was gazing. "Is your grandma okay?"

At the same time, her grandmother was repeating her name in her ear, she realized she was staring open jawed at none other than Brad Peters, but who the heck was the woman with him? "Grams, I have to go, folks are waiting on me… Yes, I love you too."

It took her a few more seconds to say her goodbyes and then she grabbed hold of her racing thoughts.

"You look an odd shade of green." Rachel continued to stare off, searching for what had triggered Jackie.

Clearing her throat, there were a couple of things she realized: first, she'd been surprised to see Brad, but nothing else. No longing, no sadness, no regrets, just confusion about who he was with. The other thing that came to her was that in only a few days, she'd grown fully at ease with Garret's sisters. Enough to tell them the truth. Or at least, some of it. "By any chance, do you know who the blonde in the pink shirt is at that back table with that man?"

Both their eyes scanned in the same general direction before the two sisters nodded their heads slightly at the same time. They were not identical twins by any stretch of the imagination, but whenever they made unified reactions like a moment ago, boy did they look like two peas in a pod.

"That's Angela Simpson," Rachel volunteered.

Jillian continued to watch the table. "You know the type—head cheerleader, Harvest Queen, and always has man candy on her arm."

"She doesn't seem to be changing her ways." Rachel studied the two people at the back table. "That guy looks like he could be on the cover of a magazine."

"So you don't know him?" Jackie asked as casually as she could.

Both heads turned from side to side.

Again, Rachel spoke first. "Definitely not from around here. You can't hide looks like that from the gossip mill."

Boy, did she have gossip to add to the mill. "His name is Brad Peters. He used to live in Houston. Now he lives in Millers Creek." Here went nothing. "With his wife."

Like a pair of matching bookends, big blue eyes rounded, surrounded by a large swath of white.

Rachel's head whipped around to face her. "Are you sure he's married?"

She didn't bother speaking, just nodded.

Her gaze narrowed, Jillian tipped her head, facing her

slowly. "And you know this how?"

This was it. "He's the reason I came to Millers Creek."

Now the two siblings blinked, raising their brows high on their foreheads, completely forgetting about the couple across the café.

"Don't stop there." Rachel's gaze remained fixed on Jackie.

"I thought he was the perfect catch. When he lost his job in Houston and had to move back to where he was from, I thought he ended things because he didn't want to subject city girl me to country living."

Patiently, their expressions blank, the two sisters waited for her to continue. At least so far, they didn't seem to be judging her.

"I got it in my head, once he saw me in his world and realized that I was happily willing to give everything up to be with him, that he'd change his mind about marriage and children and we'd live happily ever after."

"Everything?" Jillian asked carefully.

"I quit my job, sold or donated most of my things, and foolishly landed on his doorstep."

"Uh-oh." Rachel had inched closer against the table.

"Yeah. I wouldn't have even known where he lived if I hadn't found a card in the pile of mail in my kitchen. My first surprise was that he lived in a cute cottage with flowers in the window boxes. But the doozy of a start came when the woman who answered the door informed me that her husband wasn't home right then. I scrambled away as fast as I could. Found myself in the parking lot of the Bronco Lounge. I remember ordering a drink and sulking, then everything else is a blank until I woke up in a strange motel room with a note from your brother telling me to call if I needed a ride somewhere."

"He left you a note?" Rachel looked confused.

Jackie nodded. "He'd rented two rooms, one for me and one for him."

A knowing smile formed on Jillian's face. "The guy always was a goody two shoes. He scolded the heck out of Carson for knocking up Jess after a one night stand. Though

I think he was more annoyed with the one night stand part more than the baby part."

"He *was* an Eagle Scout," Rachel chimed in, the same smile on her lips.

"That would explain why having me pass out in his car didn't seem to faze him." Jackie couldn't imagine anyone else on the planet being as nice to her as Garret had been.

Jillian cocked her head to one side. "I thought you said everything that night was a blank?"

"Any information I have, came from your brother."

"Makes sense." Rachel nodded, then her gaze suddenly narrowed again. "Jackie?"

"Mm?"

"Does this Brad guy know that you know he's married?"

"I don't think so. Why?"

"Oh, nothing. Just thinking."

Just thinking. Jackie had seen a look like that in her grandmother's eyes a time or two, usually right before she'd play the card that won her the poker pot in a family card game.

CHAPTER TWELVE

Eleanor Shannon had never been one to wait for an invitation. Not back in the seventies when she'd marched in the women's rights rallies, not when she'd taken over her late husband's firm despite the skeptics, and certainly not when it came to checking up on her only granddaughter. That still small voice in the back of her head wouldn't stop asking what the heck was really going on in West Texas. She knew why her beloved grandchild had moved to Houston; as much as Eleanor loved her small hometown, Jackie couldn't wait to escape. Then, with no warning, one minute her precious Jacqueline was in Houston bubbling excitedly over a new guy in her life—Brad something—and then the next thing Eleanor knew, her big city loving granddaughter was settling down across the state in of all places, a small town. All it had taken was one short night, tossing and turning, to be packed and on the road by six am. And now, here she was.

Honeysuckle, Texas had more charm than she'd expected. She'd been picturing some dusty one-horse town with tumbleweed on the sidewalks, but the tidy storefronts and flower boxes reminded her of any number of East Texas small towns from her childhood. She parked her silver Buick—a sensible car for a not-so-sensible woman, as her friends liked to joke—and checked her lipstick in the rearview mirror. Content that she looked presentable, she stepped out of the car and began strolling down Main Street, delighted for the chance to stretch her legs and work her stiff muscles. Shop after shop tugged at her curiosity to go in and peruse, but there was only time for a quick look before she called Jackie and tracked down where she was staying.

Coming upon Corn Hole Heaven, she paused. An entire store dedicated to corn hole? Memories of playing as a child made her smile. Maybe one quick perusal wouldn't hurt anything. The bell jingled cheerfully as she pushed open the door. The interior was surprisingly spacious, filled with colorful wooden boards and fabric bags arranged by weight and color. Who knew there were so many options for accessories, and so… bright too.

"Hello!" A woman about twenty years her junior approached with a welcoming smile. "Just passing through or looking to join the corn hole revolution?"

"Neither, actually." Eleanor returned the warm smile. "My granddaughter Jacqueline recently moved to town, and I thought I'd surprise her."

The woman's face twisted in thought, then, as if a switch had been flipped, lit up like a Christmas tree. "You must mean Jackie! Oh my goodness, you're Jackie's grandmother?" She turned toward the back of the store. "Liz! Come out here! Jackie's grandmother is here!"

Another woman, clearly a sister based on their similar features, hurried from the back room.

"I'm Vicki Langley, and this is my sister Liz," the first woman explained. "We're Garret's aunts."

"Garret?" Eleanor repeated, testing the name on her tongue. Her granddaughter had been very vague about her reasons for settling into a small town—something she'd spent her entire childhood planning to escape—but this could explain a lot. A new man.

The sisters exchanged knowing glances that set off Eleanor's internal alarms.

"Jackie hasn't mentioned Garret?" Liz asked.

Eleanor shook her head.

The two siblings leaned in conspiratorially.

"He's our nephew. And, well, quite frankly," Vicki's smile took over her face, "I've never seen him so smitten."

"Smitten?" Eleanor struggled to keep her expression neutral. *Interesting. Very interesting.* So much was beginning to make sense. Sort of.

"The way he looks at her…" Vicki sighed dramatically. "It's like watching one of those old movies where the hero is absolutely besotted."

"Alice—that's Garret's mother—tells us they're together constantly," Liz added. "Laughing together in the kitchen, walking hand in hand around the ranch—"

"The ranch?"

"Why yes. Jackie is staying at the Sweet family ranch." Looking about, Liz leaned in and lowered her voice. "Just between us, he asked my sister's permission to court her."

"Court her?" Eyebrows high on her forehead, Eleanor was more confused now than ever.

The two siblings nodded in unison, both beaming like they'd found a cure for cancer.

"As in going to get married?" She hoped her voice didn't crack. So soon after her break-up with that Brad fellow in Houston, this had the earmarks of a rebound fiasco written all over it.

Again the heads bobbed enthusiastically.

Vickie rubbed her hands together with joyful enthusiasm. "We're just waiting for him to make it official."

"I see." She flashed what she hoped was a sincere smile and not that crooked one that always alerted her husband to her internal planning—or scheming as he'd called it. There might not be any scheming needed this time around, but there was certainly something cooking and she had every intention of finding out what the heck was really going on here. "Could you point me toward the ranch?"

Thumbing through the stack of seventh-grade history papers, Garret held a red pen poised above yet another creative interpretation of American history. The kitchen table made a better grading station than his bedroom—more space to spread out, and the occasional distraction of Jackie's laugh drifting in from the living room. Three times he'd caught himself smiling at the sound. Three times he'd reminded himself his arrangement with Jackie was strictly business—nothing more.

The crunch of tires on gravel pulled his attention. He wasn't expecting anyone; at this hour of the day, in the middle of the week, a surprise guest was more likely to mean someone was in trouble than wanting to socialize. Pushing back from the table, he moved across the house to the front window. A silver Buick had pulled up beside his truck, and an older woman emerged from the driver's side. Sporting pressed slacks and a light cardigan despite the Texas heat, he wondered what kind of trouble the old woman could be having. Something about her bearing—confident, purposeful—struck him as familiar.

The woman was halfway to the porch when Jackie appeared at his side. Her sharp intake of breath gave him pause. What he didn't know was if her reaction meant good news or bad.

"Grams," Jackie whispered, then louder, "Grammy!" She bolted past him, flying through the screen door and down the steps. Garret followed at a more measured pace, watching as Jackie threw her arms around the older woman. Apparently, it was safe to say his answer was good news. What he didn't know, was if this little visit meant trouble was brewing on the horizon.

"Surprise, darling," the woman said, her voice carrying a touch of East Texas in its warmth.

"What are you doing here?" Jackie pulled back, her expression flickering between joy and something that looked oddly like panic. So much for a good thing.

"Can't a grandmother check on her only grandchild?" The woman's gaze shifted to Garret, shrewd eyes taking his measure in one sweeping glance. "Especially when that grandchild suddenly moves across the state to a small town with little to no explanation."

Garret stepped forward, his shoulders straight, his smile strong. "I'm Garret Sweet. Welcome."

The woman extended her hand, her eyes never leaving his face. "Eleanor Shannon." A firm handshake, she held on a moment longer, her gaze fixed on his, scrutiny in her eyes. When she finally let go and stepped back, he had no idea where he stood, but he had a feeling the older woman had definitely come to a conclusion, he just had no idea if this was going to help or hurt their situation.

From behind, his mother called out to them. "Are y'all going to stand in the yard all day or invite our guest inside?"

"Oh, sorry. Of course." Her elbow linked with her grandmother's, Jackie led her grandmother toward the house.

"Is there a reason you haven't mentioned you're living with a handsome hunk?"

Jackie's cheeks flushed. "Grammy…"

Walking beside them, Garret tried not to smile at her grandmother's description of him. Handsome *and* a hunk. Eleanor Shannon might have just made his day.

Crossing the threshold, a wide smile bloomed on their visitor's face. "I can see why my granddaughter likes living here."

For an instant the old woman's gaze slanted in his direction, a knowing gleam in her eye, and Garret had the distinct feeling this woman was going to keep them on their toes.

Wiping her hands on a dish rag, his mother extended her hand. "Sorry for the mess. I'm in the middle of fixing supper."

Her nose to the air, Eleanor Shannon sniffed. "Cornbread?"

Alice Sweet nodded.

"Oh my, and is that… Alfredo sauce?"

His mother's smile couldn't have grown any wider. "Yes. I was busy baking all afternoon so we're having fettuccine Alfredo for dinner. You're staying, of course."

"Thank you."

"There's fresh rolls too if you prefer that to cornbread." His mother had begun walking Eleanor to the kitchen.

The woman stopped in her tracks and tipping her face up at his mother, barely shook her head. "May my grandmother Morretti forgive me, but I'll take the cornbread."

Laughing as if they'd been friends for years, the two sauntered the rest of the way to the kitchen mumbling something about marinara versus Alfredo and linguini and angel hair pasta.

"Are we in trouble?" he mouthed softly to Jackie.

With a lazy shrug, she rolled her head. "I have no idea."

The sound of spitting gravel caught both their attention, followed by a car door slamming and booted heels stomping up the porch steps. Another moment and the screen door flew open.

Eyes wide as saucers and slightly out of breath from the jaunt to the house, Rachel zeroed in on Jackie. "You. Will. Not. Believe this."

"Believe what?" Her gaze narrowed, Jackie swung around to face his sister.

"I bumped into Iris Hathaway at the candle shop. She was telling Jillian all about Angela Simpson's handsome new… ready?… Fiancé!"

"Oh, no." Jackie's hand flew to her mouth. "Brad proposed to her?"

Hands fisted on her hips, Rachel dipped her chin down and up. "Ooooh, yes."

Brad was engaged? Jackie's stomach twisted as she processed Rachel's words. To the blonde from the café? What scam was this character thinking he could pull off? Did he really intend to become a bigamist and drive back and forth between two wives, or did he have some other crazy scheme up his sleeve? "Are we sure she's not just hopeful?"

Rachel nodded vigorously. "According to Iris, he proposed last night. Got down on one knee and everything."

Garret followed them, his expression darkening. "This guy gets worse by the minute."

The three of them sank onto the couch, Jackie's mind racing. Disbelief at Brad's audacity simmered until pure anger at his nerve brewed to a boil. "I need to tell his wife."

"Well, someone needs to tell Angela before she gets in any deeper." Rachel leaned forward eagerly. "This man can't just keep collecting women like trading cards."

"What man collects women like trading cards?" Grams' voice made all three of them jump. She stood in the doorway, her glance drifting to Garret, then back to her granddaughter.

"Grams, I—" Jackie started, but her grandmother raised a hand.

"I couldn't help but overhear. These old ears still work remarkably well." She crossed the room and perched on the arm of the sofa beside Jackie. "Would this be the same Brad you were so smitten with in Houston?"

Jackie nodded.

"And he skipped over marrying you and chose this woman here in town?"

Again, Jackie bobbed her head, wondering how she'd gotten so lucky to have dodged a marriage proposal from Brad. "There's a bigger problem."

Her grandmother's brows drifted high on her forehead, but she sat silently waiting for what Jackie had to say.

"He already has a wife," Rachel blurted out.

Immediately Grams eyes narrowed in disbelief, and then just as quickly her chin lifted, eyes sparkling with mischief. It was the same look Grams had when she'd accidentally poisoned the shrubs a neighbor had planted— and refused to move—from their side of the property line, or when her police buddies cited Joe Parker with a traffic violation over and over for an entire month after smacking her best friend's granddaughter. Yep, she'd seen that look a lot throughout her childhood whenever her grandmother saw injustice and was brewing an idea to help Karma along. Grams tapped her fingers against her knee. "You know, when I was in college, there was a boy who tried to date three girls from the same sorority house."

"What happened?" Garret asked.

"Let's just say some lessons need to be taught publicly to really stick." Her smile broadened. "And Mary Jo Pucket's brother looks really good in makeup and a padded bra."

Stifling a chuckle, Rachel leaned forward. "Mrs. Shannon, I think I would have liked going to college with you."

"It's Eleanor, dear, and likewise."

"So," Jackie inched forward in her seat, "does this mean we're going to help teach Brad a lesson"?

Pushing to her feet, her grandmother looked at the three of them. "Sometimes, helping karma along can be an awfully entertaining way to pass the time."

CHAPTER THIRTEEN

Pushing scrambled eggs around her plate, Jackie's fork scraped against the dish in the otherwise quiet kitchen. Garret wished there was something he could do or say to take away the weight that Jackie carried since learning Brad was a serial stinker. Usually, Saturday morning breakfast at the ranch meant pancakes stacked high, bacon crisp and plentiful, and conversation flowing freely. Today, everyone privy to the plans for the day seemed just a tad off kilter.

His mother refilled coffee cups without comment.

"So," he broke the silence as Rachel checked her watch for the third time in ten minutes, "what time are you two heading into town?"

Rachel set her empty mug down with a decisive thunk. "As soon as Jackie finishes pretending to eat."

"I'm not pretending. I'm thinking." Jackie abandoned any effort at eating and pushed her plate away. "And I've pretty much run out of thoughts. Time to hit the road."

Garret leaned forward, lowering his voice even though his mother had disappeared into the pantry. "Are you sure you want to do this?"

The determination in Jackie's eyes gave him his answer before she spoke. "I have to. I just keep thinking, if someone had warned me about Brad back in Houston, I could have avoided a lot of heartache. Angela deserves the same chance."

Something twisted in Garret's chest—admiration, maybe, or something deeper he wasn't ready to name. "I'm just trying to figure out what this guy's endgame is. He can't possibly be planning to be a bigamist, shuttling between two towns and two wives."

"I've been wondering the same thing," Jackie tucked a strand of hair behind her ear. "Why propose to Angela when he never even hinted at marriage with me? I mean, even if shuffling between two families from Millers Creek to Honeysuckle is easier than between West Texas and Houston, none of this makes sense."

Rachel snorted. "Maybe Angela has money."

"Does she?" Jackie's forehead creased in thought. "But that makes me wonder—does his wife have money?"

"Could be why he stays married." Garret hefted a shoulder in a brief shrug. "Keep the financial security of one relationship while pursuing others on the side."

"Maybe…" Jackie nodded slowly. "But why go so far as proposing? Why not string her along like he did with me?"

"We can speculate all day, or we can get moving and find our answers." Rachel stood, slinging her purse over her shoulder. "Ready to go?"

Jackie took a deep breath, squared her shoulders. "Ready as I'll ever be."

Garret rose as they did. Something compelled him to reach for Jackie's hand as she passed, stopping her with a gentle tug. "Call me if you need back up."

Her smile softened, eyes warming. "I will. But entertaining Grams, showing her around the ranch and the animals, that's the best help you can give me today."

The urge to go with her, to protect her from a potentially outraged woman—or worse, an unscrupulous ex—was stronger than he'd expected. Without thinking, he leaned in and brushed his lips lightly against hers. "For luck," he murmured, pulling back just enough to see surprise flicker across her face.

A throat cleared behind them, and Garret turned to find his mother standing in the kitchen doorway, a dish towel in hand and a knowing smile on her face, her eyes settled on their still-joined hands.

Jackie's cheeks flushed pink as she squeezed his fingers once before letting go.

"You girls have a good time in town," his mom called out. "And don't worry about Eleanor; we'll take good care of her."

"Thank you. We won't be long." Jackie's gaze lingered a moment longer, locked with his, before she slipped out the door with Rachel close behind.

As the screen door swung shut, his mother's smile widened. "That girl's good for you," she said simply, before turning back to the kitchen.

Garret remained at the window, watching Jackie and Rachel climb into Rachel's car. He told himself he was playing his part well—the devoted boyfriend seeing his girl off. The uncomfortable truth, settling like a weight in his chest, was that less and less of it felt like acting anymore.

The rhinestone-studded "OPEN" sign in the window of Shear Perfection glinted against the morning sunlight as Rachel pushed open the door. A bell tinkled overhead, announcing their arrival to the salon's lone occupant.

Angela Simpson looked up from behind the reception counter, her blonde hair swept into a perfect updo, engagement ring sparkling as she waved. "Good morning, Rachel." She turned to face her morning appointment. "You must be Jackie. I've got the coffee brewing."

The salon was small but stylish—three stations with large mirrors, black leather chairs, and a row of hair dryers along one wall. Photos of smiling clients sporting Angela's handiwork lined another wall, interspersed with framed cosmetology certificates. A small "Owner/Stylist" placard sat on Angela's station.

"Can I get either of you something to drink?" Large pink mug in hand, Angela moved toward the coffee station.

"Just water for me." Jackie's voice sounded much steadier than she felt.

Rachel shook her head. "I'm fine, thanks."

Inhaling a long sip of coffee, Angela smiled and waved

Jackie to her styling chair, and setting the mug down on top of a rolling tray at her side, she draped the black cape around Jackie's shoulders with practiced ease. "So we're thinking a trim today? Maybe some layers?" Her fingers raked through Jackie's hair as she assessed it in the mirror.

"Just a trim." Jackie met Angela's eyes in the reflection, gathering her courage. "Actually, Angela, we didn't just come for a haircut."

Angela's hands paused momentarily before resuming their work. "Oh? What's up?"

Rachel moved closer, positioning herself where Angela could see her. "It's about Brad."

"Brad?" Angela's smile brightened, her left hand held out, fingers wiggling for the impressive ring to catch the light. "Isn't it gorgeous? He said he had it custom-made."

The pride in Angela's voice made Jackie's stomach clench. She recognized that feeling—the certainty that you'd been chosen by someone special, someone who saw your worth.

"Angela," Jackie watched the hairdresser through the mirror, "how long have you known Brad?"

"Almost eight months now." Angela reached for her scissors.

Eight months? Jackie bit down on her back teeth. The sleaze wasn't just two-timing her, he was three timing her.

"He comes to town regularly for work," Angela continued. "The first time he walked in here for a haircut, I just knew there was something special about him." She laughed. "I'm not usually so forward, but I wrote my number on his receipt."

Rachel leaned against the empty styling station. "And he told you he was single?"

"Of course he did." Angela's hands froze mid-motion. "What kind of question is that?"

Jackie swallowed hard. "The kind you ask when you know he's not."

The salon went completely silent except for the soft hum of the air conditioning. Angela's face in the mirror shifted from confusion to defensiveness.

"What exactly are you saying?" Angela was no longer bothering to attempt to style Jackie's hair.

"Recently, I met his wife." Hopefully, she wouldn't have to share all the humiliating details from when she discovered the truth. Though, when this was all behind them, she should probably thank Brad for his part in her meeting Garret.

Angela's laugh was sharp and disbelieving. "That's ridiculous. You must be thinking of another Brad. Mine has never been married."

"Your Brad," arms crossed, Rachel stared at Angela, "drives a fire-red Maserati, claims to work in corporate consulting—"

"And," Jackie interrupted her newest friend and future—if only temporarily—sister-in-law, "he has a small scar on his left shoulder from a childhood accident."

Angela's face paled slightly. "How do you know about his car? And his scar?"

Jackie met her eyes in the mirror. "Because I dated him too."

"I don't believe you." It was hard to say what trembled more, Angela's voice or her hands. "This is crazy. I think you should leave."

"I wish it wasn't true," Jackie said. "But look."

Jackie scrolled through her phone before flipping it around and showing a photo of Jackie and Brad standing beside his distinctive red sports car, his arm wrapped possessively around her waist. The date stamp showed it was taken just two months ago.

"That's… that doesn't mean anything." Uncertainty had crept into Angela's voice.

"There's more." Jackie swiped to the next image—a screenshot of property records for Millers Creek that Rachel had found after hearing about the latest engagement, with Bradley and Diane Peters listed as joint owners of a house on Magnolia Lane.

Angela set the scissors down carefully on the counter, her fingers white-knuckled. "There has to be an explanation."

"I thought so too," Jackie admitted. "When I showed up at his house in Millers Creek and his wife answered the door, I spent hours trying to come up with explanations that would make it not true."

"His wife?" Angela whispered, sinking onto the adjacent styling chair. "No. He can't be..." Her voice trailed off as she stared at the evidence on Jackie's phone.

"I'm so sorry." Jackie heaved an unsteady sigh. "I know exactly how you're feeling right now."

A tear slipped down Angela's cheek, leaving a trail in her perfectly applied makeup. "I don't understand. We've started planning our wedding. He's meeting with a realtor next week to find us a place. Why would he—" She broke off, twisting the engagement ring on her finger. "Oh God. I have a trust fund from my grandmother. It's how I bought the salon. He said he'd help me invest it so it grows stronger."

Jackie reached across, laying her hand over Angela's trembling fingers. "I truly am sorry, but I know if it were me, I'd want someone to tell me what was going on."

Angela stared at their joined hands for a long moment, her shoulders slumping. Then gradually, her posture straightened. "I might need a good character witness after I kill him. You girls up for the job?"

"Actually," Rachel chuckled softly, "we were hoping you might like to join us."

"Join you?" Confusion had returned to Angela's face.

Jackie grinned. "As my Grams has often said, revenge can be bittersweet, but karma can be pure entertainment. We thought it might be fun to move karma along. Care to join the fun?"

CHAPTER FOURTEEN

Rachel drummed her fingers against the steering wheel, eyeing the tidy brick home across the street. They'd been sitting here for twenty minutes, no closer to a concrete plan than when they'd left Honeysuckle. A sleek silver Mercedes sat in the driveway. Unless the guy kept a sports car and a practical car, it had to belong to the wife.

"So," she glanced sideways at Jackie in the passenger seat and Angela hunched forward from the back, "now what?"

"We ring the doorbell and tell her the truth?" Jackie's words lacked conviction.

Angela snorted. "Right. 'Hi, you don't know us, but your husband proposed to me last week, and broke up with her not long before that. Want to help us destroy him?'"

"When you put it that way…" Jackie winced.

"Maybe we should just—" Rachel stopped mid-sentence, straightening in her seat. "She's coming out."

A slim woman with shoulder-length blonde hair stepped out the front door, locking it behind her. She wore white capris and a navy blouse, looking every bit the polished suburban wife.

"That's her." Jackie slinked down in her seat. "That's who answered the door when I showed up looking for Brad."

"Looks like he has a type." Rachel's gaze narrowed on the casually elegant woman as she slid into her car. "Tall, blonde, and confident."

"Never in my life have I looked that confident." Jackie

straightened in her seat as the car backed out of the driveway.

"So. I repeat, now what?"

"Follow her." Jackie pointed. "Maybe if we get an idea what she's like it will help us decide how to deal with her."

Rachel had her doubts but it made more sense than sitting here watching an empty house waiting for the wife—or worse, Brad—to return. "Just so we're clear, if she spots us and calls the police, I'm throwing you both under the bus."

Following the luxury sedan, Rachel tried not to get too close, and prayed the woman didn't notice them on her tail. A few more miles and the Mercedes signaled and turned into the parking lot of the Harvest Market grocery store.

"Perfect," Angela whispered as Rachel found a spot several spaces away. "Grocery stores are great for casual run-ins."

"Because nothing says *casual* like three women following you down the cereal aisle," Rachel muttered, but she found herself caught up in the absurdity of their mission.

Inside, they grabbed a shopping basket as cover and spotted their target examining organic produce.

Grabbing a shopping cart, Rachel looked to the woman who would soon be her next sister-in-law. "So what exactly are we hoping to learn from this mission?"

Stopping a few feet behind Brad's wife, Rachel feigned interest in how much sugar was on the label of the first can she'd grabbed. Too bad the label gave her no clue to what she was holding. Maybe it was time to find her grandmother's canning recipes.

"There she goes." Jackie and Angela quickly placed the products they were not really interested in back in the cart.

In the baking aisle, Rachel tossed a bag of ordinary white flour in the basket, noting that Mrs. Brad purchased almond flour. Further down the aisle, the woman in their sites carefully perused the sugar section.

Muttering through closed teeth, Angela leaned into her two cohorts. "What's so difficult about buying sugar?"

Stealing a gaze down the aisle, Rachel squinted at the product the tall blonde had placed in her cart. "Coconut palm sugar."

"You get sugar from coconuts?" Angela fell into step beside the cart.

With a casual shrug, Jackie hurried on Rachel's other side. "Apparently."

"Who knew?" Angela sighed. "I'm getting a clearer picture on why this woman looks so... sleek."

"I may have to cut back on Alice's cinnamon rolls," Jackie mumbled to no one in particular.

Rachel understood. Working from sun up to sun down on a ranch helped keep the calories in check, but sitting behind a desk three days a week did little to keep the sweet tooth pounds at bay.

They continued up and down the aisles behind this woman. She preferred organic fruits and vegetables, clearly liked to bake, believed in storing up her omega fatty acids with plenty of fresh fish, not only preferred almond flour, but also almond milk and the frozen food aisle was not on her radar. Unfortunately, none of this gave an inkling of why Brad Peters was two, or was it three timing her? Or of how the woman would react when she learned about her hubby's extra-curricular activity. And none of it gave any indication of whether or not she'd want to join the rest of them in teaching her husband a well-deserved lesson.

As the wife went through the check out lane, the three spies hurried quickly through a nearby lane, their attention on the woman.

"Did she just pay for all that with cash?" Angela asked.

Looking over, Jackie nodded. "I guess they're not cash poor."

"At least she isn't," Rachel commented.

Doing their best not to draw attention to themselves, they strolled out of the store, practically tossed the bags of groceries they didn't need into the rear of the car and belted themselves in. The silver Mercedes was still parked a few spaces over, but no sign of the wife.

"Where did she go?" Jackie leaned forward, scanning

the lot in front of them.

Looking over her shoulder, Rachel squinted at the sun. "How could we lose her? She was right there."

A tap sounded on the front passenger window and the three of them whipped their heads to the right.

Diane Peters stood at the side, her fingers waving like a mom entertaining a toddler, her smile as plastic as the credit card she didn't use.

Quickly, Rachel hit the button to lower the window.

Once the glass disappeared into the door, the woman's smile slipped. "Who the hell are you people and why have you been following me?" Her free hand shifted her purse in front of her. "And if you're wondering," her hand gently tapped the side of her luxury brand leather purse, "I carry more than cash in this baby."

"Whoa." Jackie held up both hands; this was definitely not the way she'd expected the day to go. Certainly not having a pistol-toting ticked off wife confronting them. "We're not here to cause trouble."

"Really?" The upset woman's eyebrow arched perfectly. "Three women stalking me through a grocery store, then racing out to your car to watch me? What exactly would you call that?"

Angela leaned forward from the back seat. "We're the other women."

"Well," Rachel shrugged one shoulder, "not me, them."

Diane's perfectly composed expression faltered for just a moment. "Excuse me?"

"I'm Jackie Drake." Thankfully, Jackie's voice sounded steadier than she'd expected knowing there was an angry woman inches away from her with a loaded gun handy. "I dated your husband in Houston until I found out he was married."

"You came to the house." Anger slowly shifted to confusion as brows buckled, Diane stared at her.

Jackie nodded. "That would be when I learned Brad was married."

"And I'm Angela Simpson." Angela pressed fully against the front-row seats. "Your husband proposed to me last week. I live in Honeysuckle."

Diane's face cycled through confusion, disbelief, and then—unexpectedly—resignation. She glanced around the parking lot.

"I'm sorry if we've hurt you." Jackie latched onto the shock she felt when she'd found out Brad was already married. "But we felt you needed to know what's happening; I just hadn't meant to blurt it out in a public parking lot."

Closing her eyes a moment, Diane nodded. "All right. You've done your good deed for the day. I'll take it from here."

"Actually," Jackie straightened in her seat, "we were thinking more along the lines of helping you—and karma—along."

Her gaze narrowing as she studied Jackie's face, she seemed to weigh the truth of her words. Then, offering an almost imperceptible nod of her head, her stance eased and her hand fell from her handbag to her side. "I'm listening."

Jackie turned left then right, taking in every passing shopper in the parking lot. "Perhaps we could do this somewhere else?"

"You look more nervous than a cat in a room full of rockers." Jackie's grandmother sat at the kitchen table, enjoying her lunch with his mom and brothers.

The fork in Garret's mom's hand stilled halfway to her mouth. "Did something go wrong with the irrigation system?"

"Nope," Preston answered. "Small patch job set everything right again."

His mom's shoulders relaxed a moment before she

stiffened again. "A problem with the fence lines?"

This time Carson looked up. "Everything's fine, Mom. Why are you suddenly so spooked?"

His mother looked from Jackie's grandmother to Garret and back. "Eleanor is right. Garret looks like he's sitting in a room of rattlers waiting to strike."

His mom's analogy was closer to the truth than Eleanor's. For all he knew, Brad's wife Diane might very well strike like a rattler and that thought had him more than a bit unsettled. He'd hoped to hear from them by now. If not a call, a text, anything to let him know things were not going to hell in a hand basket. "I'm just thinking about some challenges at school. I'll figure it out."

"I see." His mom studied him a moment before accepting her son's reply and returning to her lunch.

As if everyone's concern had summoned Jackie, his phone dinged with a text. *All is good. We're on our way back to town.*

A moment later, Eleanor's phone buzzed. The older woman continued to eat, ignoring her phone. While he admired her determination to avoid the distractions of cell phones when eating or visiting with folks, right about now he wanted to know if Jackie had more news for them.

Another minute or so and his phone dinged again. Another text from Jackie. *Tell Grams to meet us at Heaven Scent. Jillian is expecting everyone.*

Everyone? Who was everyone and why were they meeting at Jillian's candle shop?

Another text came through. *You too.*

Well, at least maybe now he'd get some answers. What he wasn't so sure of, was whether or not he would like any of what he was going to learn.

CHAPTER FIFTEEN

"I think you've all lost your minds." Bright and early, before he'd had enough coffee to clear his head, Garret simply shook his head at his brothers, their wives, his sisters, and Jackie, all gathered in his Dad's office. "It's one thing to tell the principal parties involved of Brad's unscrupulous behavior, but it's something totally different to gang up on him."

"Why?" Arms crossed, Rachel sat in the lone recliner.

"Because it could backfire on all of you." From the determined look on the faces of the women in his life, Garret knew he was wasting his breath, but he had to try.

"Garret has a point." Carson looked at his sister Jillian, whose body language mimicked her twin's. "No one has any idea how Brad will react, or how much trouble he can cause if he chooses to get even."

Scanning the room, it was clear, the women stood on the side of insanity and the men did not.

"We spent all of last night coming up with a detailed plan," Jackie explained.

"And with today being the Annual Corn Hole School Fundraising Festival, it's the perfect time to pull it off. It will be fun." Jackie smiled at him.

"Fun?" the three men in the room echoed.

"You'll see. We've got this." Rachel spoke, but also sporting a satisfied grin, Jillian nodded with her twin.

Nothing about this sat well with Garret, but it was pretty clear to him and his brothers, this was one battle they weren't going to win. Glancing down at his watch, just a couple more hours and Operation Pay Back was about to begin.

In full swing, slightly past noon, the Honeysuckle Annual Corn Hole Festival to support school funding pulsed with life. Laughter mingled with the twang of country music, the rhythmic thud of beanbags, and the tempting scent of popcorn and grilled onions. Garret kept a watchful eye on the happenings, his gaze flicking between Jackie—standing near the raffle booth with Rachel and Jillian, projecting an air of breezy nonchalance—and Angela, who having assured the precious Maserati was parked as planned in front of the cafe, strolled along with Brad Peters smugly attached to her arm.

There was no way Garret or anyone else could miss how utterly out of place Brad looked amidst the small-town charm. Wearing crisp chinos and according to everything the women had told him, his clearly overpriced, custom-made Italian loafers, Brad radiated misplaced importance.

Earlier that morning, before taking their designated places, Diane had pressed a small, familiar key into Jackie's hand. Grim satisfaction shone in her eyes. Garret knew the plans that the women had concocted at the candle shop last night, but somehow seeing it all slowly come to life had his stomach twisted in knots. These women might consider this little karma plot all fun and games, but Garret was not at all convinced.

Now, as Angela steered Brad towards the funnel cake stand, Jackie palmed the key to Jillian. A shared look of understanding passed between them, before each woman went their separate ways, the passing crowds oblivious to anything but good food and toe-tapping music.

"Operation Payback is a go," as Rachel pretended to admire a quilt, her voice murmured into everyone's ear. Each of them wore one ear bud, the group call already live before they split up—no texting, no fumbling with phones.

Garret almost wished he weren't privy to the blow-by-blow commentaries. Instead, he stood casually near Jackie's grandmother and his mother at a prime picnic table, perfectly positioned to observe. And pounce, if needed.

Grams, adjusting her floppy sun hat, gave a subtle nod to her co-conspirators. "Isn't this lovely, Alice?" Eleanor beamed. "So much community spirit."

"It certainly is," his mom agreed, pointing. "Oh look, there's Angela with her young man. Garret, didn't you say Jackie knew him from Houston?"

"Briefly, Mom. Small world." Garret forced a smile, his gaze fixed on his kid sister. His stomach tightened. This whole plan felt like juggling dynamite.

Jillian, who had opted to leave the candle shop in an employee's hands in order to participate in the mission, meandered towards the parking lot. With every *doo doo, doo doo*, her choice to hum the theme from *Mission Impossible* in everyone's ears did nothing to calm the knots tightening in his gut.

A few minutes later, she reappeared near the lemonade stand, catching Rachel's eye with a discreet thumbs-up. Softly she muttered to the group, "Phase one executed flawlessly, if I do say so myself."

Brad's flashy red Maserati previously parked in front of the café doors, now occupied the spot directly in front of the fire hydrant.

Oblivious to the shenanigans planned by the women in his life, Brad sampled a piece of fudge Angela offered. "Quite good, for local fare," his voice dripped with condescension. Then eyes bulging, fudge at his lips, he froze.

Garret knew exactly what had caught the poor schmuck's attention. Diane stood nearby chatting easily with Aunt Vicki near the Corn Hole Heaven tent.

Panic flickered in Brad's eyes. "You know, darling..." He spun quickly, taking Angela's arm, not knowing everyone could hear him thanks to the phone in Angela's purse. "I suddenly have a craving to see... animals. Didn't you say you wanted to visit the petting zoo?"

Beautifully, Angela feigned surprise, then delight. "Oh, yes! The bunnies are adorable. Come on."

She practically dragged Brad towards the penned-off

area where Clint, volunteering for the day and in on the plans, was diligently mucking out the goat enclosure. For a man who supposedly wanted to see animals, Brad's nose twitched with distaste and his gaze seemed to search for a quick exit route.

"Oh, Brad. Aren't they precious?" Angela cooed, pointing at a particularly fluffy goat. "Stand right here, the light catches your profile perfectly. Let me get a picture." Phone held high, she frowned, then nudged him a tad to the left, positioning him precisely on a clean thin patch of straw.

Odors forgotten, Brad puffed out his chest, striking a pose.

Taking a step to the side, angling the camera, she paused, waving madly as if just noticing who was working the pens. "Hi, Clint!"

Shovel in hand, the Sweet's lone ranch hand Clint, as if genuinely startled by the greeting, straightened and turned abruptly towards the sound of Angela's voice. The shovel, laden with wet, fragrant goat manure, swung in a wide arc.

Splat. A generous dollop landed squarely across the toes of Brad's pristine, hand-stitched loafers. Another glob splattered onto his chinos for good measure. Yep, X had indeed marked the perfect spot.

"Whoa there!" Clint grunted, feigning surprise. "Sorry 'bout that, mister. Guess I swung when I should have stopped." He casually scraped the remaining manure into the wheelbarrow.

Brad stared down at his feet, his face contorting in growing fury. The smell hit him, thick and earthy, and he gagged slightly. "My shoes! These are bespoke! Do you have any idea—"

"Oh, Brad! Honey! Are you okay?" Angela rushed over, photo forgotten, dabbing uselessly at his shoe with a tissue.

"Terrible luck." Alice Sweet called out, having ambled over with Eleanor to see the animals.

Eleanor surveyed the scene, a faint smile playing on her lips. "Accidents do happen, dear. Especially when one isn't paying attention."

Brad, trying futilely to scrape the offending muck from his shoes on a patch of grass, looked up to see Diane approaching calmly from one side. Spinning away, his eyes darting about like a trapped rat looking for escape, he spotted Jackie approaching from the other direction. His face went from furious red to clammy white. The guy was cornered.

"Brad? Having some trouble?" Diane asked mildly, taking in the state of his shoes with detached interest.

"Diane...Wha, what are you doing here?" Subtly he tried to shift so Angela wasn't directly in Diane's line of sight.

"Brad!" Jackie exclaimed with forced cheerfulness. "What a surprise seeing you here. Enjoying the local... uh... atmosphere?" She wrinkled her nose slightly.

He looked frantically between his composed wife and his smiling ex.

"Everything all right here, honey?" Angela stepped closer to Brad again, completing the triangle of women surrounding him.

As Brad, utterly flustered and hemmed in, stuttered to find words, Rachel materialized holding two enormous Sno-Cones, dripping with luridly blue and sticky-red syrup.

"Coming through!" Rachel called out, swerving about like the town drunk, evading low scrambling critters, and with a dramatic flair worthy of an Academy Award, proceeded to lose her balance, stumbling directly into his path.

The blue Sno-Cone met Brad's neatly pressed white tailored shirt, leaving a massive, rapidly spreading stain. The red iced treat made glancing contact with his perfectly styled hair, depositing a sticky, melting glob near his temple.

"Oh, my stars! I am *so* sorry!" Rachel gasped, dropping the now-empty paper cones. "They're just so slippery! Are you okay?"

Brad sputtered, trying to swipe the sticky syrup from his hair, only smearing it further. He looked down at the vibrant blue and red masterpiece blooming across his shirt, dripping down his paint leg, and onto his manure-caked shoes. His face was a thundercloud.

"First manure, now Sno-Cones." Alice shook her head as she and Eleanor caught up. "This poor young man is having the worst day."

"Indeed." Eleanor's eyes sparkling with amusement. "Almost seems like the universe is trying to tell him something."

Attracted to the sweet scent of syrupy ice, every four-legged animal within the pen raced in his direction. One goat merrily chewed on a loafer tassel—amazing that goats could eat anything no matter what they were covered in—while another licked at his pants. Soon baby lambs and bunnies surrounded him, all interested in an early-afternoon snack.

Garret had to admit, the ladies couldn't have pulled this off more smoothly had they been professional stuntmen. The coordination was precise and the results… entertaining.

It was at that precise moment, with Brad looking like a Jackson Pollock painting attacked by farm animals, that the unmistakable rumble of a truck echoed from the road, red and blue lights to match his stained clothing beginning their rhythmic flash.

Kicking at the growing menagerie of animals at his heels, and swiping at the syrup sticky mess dripping from his hair, Brad glanced up to see the…"Tow truck?" His eyes widened in fresh horror as the driver began hooking the truck to his Maserati. Galloping to the curb, animals, manure, and sticky mess forgotten, he came to a screeching halt by the drive. "That's my car!"

"Shouldn't have parked it in a fire lane," the tow truck driver yelled back calmly.

His head whipping left to where the car should have been and then right to where the tow truck driver connected a hook with his precious car, Brad's gaze narrowed, the muscle in his jaw twitched and through gritted teeth, he argued, "I'll pay the ticket. Just unhook it."

"Sorry sir, you'll have to deal with the county judge to

get your car back."

Brad fumbled for his wallet and pulled out a hundred dollar bill, waving it at the driver. "Surely we can come to an understanding."

"Something wrong here?" The sheriff strolled to a stop at the passenger's side.

"I believe this man," the driver pointed at Brad, "intends to bribe me into not towing his car."

"Is he?" The sheriff crossed his arms and stared pointedly at Brad.

Slowly putting his wallet back in his pocket, Brad shook his head. "No, sir. Wouldn't think of it."

The sheriff slapped the driver on the back. "You have a good day, Bill."

"Same to you, Sheriff."

The officer tipped his hat at the ladies and continued down the sidewalk.

Standing in what had been his parking spot, his gaze lingering on the tail end of his precious car as the rear fender jolted over a bump in the road, even from where he stood, Garret could hear Brad wince, seconds before whirling around to face the three women. "This is all your doing."

A crisp, legal-sized envelope in hand, Diane waved it at him.

"What's this?" His gaze focused on the manila envelope much the way he might stare at a rattler about to strike.

"Divorce papers." Diane's steadiness, and smile, didn't falter. Garret didn't bother to ask what kind of connections the woman had to have the papers drawn up and ready in less than twenty-four hours.

"Diane, sweetie. You don't mean that. We love each other."

Her one brow rose high above her eye. "Brad, you wouldn't have a clue what love was if it bit you in the ass."

"That's not true." He stepped forward as if forgetting his paramours were watching with ringside seats.

Taking a step back, Diane shook her head. "Our prenup was very clear about infidelity. All assets acquired during the marriage—which we both know I paid for anyhow—remain with the faithful party."

"And that," Jackie smiled, "would not be you."

Brad blinked as if suddenly remembering his audience.

"You'll find our sworn affidavits attesting to your... uh... extracurricular activities in the envelope." Angela waved in Diane's direction. "Oh, and I get to keep the ring."

The blood drained from Brad's face. He looked to where his beloved car had been parked only moments ago, then down to the manure cementing itself to his thousand-dollar shoes, the vibrant Sno-Cone art decorating his shirt and hair, the divorce papers signaling his financial ruin, and the three women watching him. The crowd was hushed, phones held aloft.

"You... you set me up." He finally choked out.

Eleanor Shannon glided forward, adjusting her hat. "Set you up? Heavens no, young man. It simply appears your chickens... or perhaps in this case, your goats... and your Sno-Cones... have come home to roost." She surveyed the scene. "Quite spectacularly, I might add."

"So the sheriff wasn't part of the plan?" Carson asked.

"Nope." Jackie couldn't help grinning. "That was sheer dumb luck that he tried to bribe the driver just as the sheriff passed by."

"My favorite, though," Jillian bit back a laugh, "was Clint's perfect aim. I was so worried that Brad would notice the x tape under the straw."

Jess set the pitcher of sweet tea on the table. "Well, I think y'all did a great job."

Diane and Angela, having joined the family for a celebratory of sorts dinner, nodded.

"I keep asking myself what I ever saw in him in the first place," Angela said as she refilled her glass.

"Tell me about it," Diane echoed.

"Now, none of that." Alice Sweet stood with a warm

blueberry pie in hand. "The man was a skilled scammer. No one's fault that he charmed everyone."

"She's right." Jackie nodded. It had taken a while for them to put all the pieces together. Apparently holding down a job long term was not Brad's strength. Having a wife with money was more of a necessity for him than a perk. More than once, Diane had threatened him with divorce if he didn't straighten up. Jackie had most likely been nothing more than a fun diversion, but they suspected Angela was his next meal ticket if Diane followed through with her threats. "I've heard of exes becoming friends, but didn't think it would be this much fun."

"Fun," Garret muttered. "There were a couple of times when I thought for sure the guy was going to retaliate and I'd wind up in jail for manslaughter."

On the grand scheme of romantic things Jackie had dreamed of hearing, that had not been one of them, and yet, for her, it was the most romantic thing she'd ever heard.

"Don't look so surprised." Her grandmother slid a warm slice of pie in front of her. "The boy loves you."

She glanced over at him. Cheeks slightly flushed, his hands in his pockets, and his gaze locking with hers, he straightened his shoulders, nodded, and Jackie's heart melted in her chest. Garret Lamar Sweet loved her. Really loved her.

CHAPTER SIXTEEN

A whirlwind of a day was the understatement of the year. Every minute of the day, right up until Diane paid for a ride to take Brad back to their house, where he was given twenty-four hours to pack his personal belongings and find somewhere else to live, Garret had been on edge.

Not that Jackie was in any danger of serious injury, but Garret didn't want a single hair on her head, or beat of her heart, hurt, and today promised any of the above possible. In too many ways to list.

Now, much to his surprise, he'd confessed, sort of, to loving Jackie for real. Not a ploy to save the ranch, not a charade to fool his mother, but honestly, truly, and deeply, loved Jackie. As in the put a ring on her finger and treasure her for the rest of their lives kind of love. All he had to do was convince her to make their little game real.

"I love how bright the stars are out here." Jackie's grandmother glanced out the kitchen window. "We had night skies like that when I was a little girl, but not anymore. Too much growth and light pollution."

"It's one of the many things I love about being out here," Jackie cast a sideways glance at Garret before returning her gaze to her grandmother.

"If y'all will excuse me a minute," Garret pushed away from the table, "I need to run upstairs. I'll be right back."

Some heads nodded, but the conversation around the table continued as if he were still there. With one exception, he could feel Jackie's gaze on him all the way to the stairs. All he could think was, now or never.

Resisting the urge to take the steps two at a time, he

eased up the staircase and made his way directly to his room. Closing the door behind him, he slowly opened the top dresser drawer. Hidden inside a pair of white athletic socks, he slid out the simple black velvet box. Taking a moment to lift it open, the solitaire ring sparkled under the overhead light.

The ring had been a splurge. When he and his siblings had decided to seek out temporary marriages, he'd thought to only purchase a simple wedding band for his fake bride. Once Jackie came into the picture, he'd not given the rings any more thought until the day last week when he'd found himself at the jewelers. Somehow, a simple band alone didn't feel right. This solitaire had caught his eye.

A small swirl of gold around the main stone with a tiny diamond encircled at either side had seemed a perfect fit for Jackie. The main diamond, tough enough to stand the test of time. The surrounding design, delicate and whimsical, and reminded him very much of Jackie. Without hesitation, he'd put the ring on his credit card and then brought it home and buried it in the drawer.

Tucking it away in his pocket, sans the sock, he said a small prayer that the look he'd seen in her eyes a few minutes ago meant what he thought it did. That there was a real chance for them. And not just for a single year. Taking the steps downstairs at a measured pace, he returned to the dining room. Voices merry with success bounced back and forth. Jackie sat quietly taking it all in. He willed his heart to stop pounding for fear the whole room would hear it as clearly as he did.

Not wanting to draw attention to his intent, he leaned over Jackie's shoulder and lowering his voice, whispered, "Join me outside a minute."

Smiling up at him, she nodded, set her napkin on the table and the two slipped out of the room.

"Is anything wrong?" She glanced down at the hand that now held hers and was leading her through the kitchen and out the back door onto the porch.

"Not at all." He was hoping something—no, everything—was perfectly right. Looking over his shoulder to ensure no one had thought to follow them, he stood at her side, leaning against the porch railing. "Your grandmother's right. It's a beautiful night."

"They all are." Her chin lifted, her smile sweet, her gaze settled on the tapestry above of bright lights on dark velvet.

To him, she was more beautiful than the West Texas sky.

"I know I haven't been here long, but I can't imagine living in the big city again." Her hands squeezed the railing as she leaned back slightly. "For one thing, this no rush hour traffic is way better than I imagined."

He couldn't help but chuckle. "That's true."

"And having everyone know your business isn't nearly as bad as it's made out to be in the movies."

That much he wasn't so sure of, though they had used it to their advantage the last few months while trying to save the ranch.

"Have you ever thought of living anywhere else?" Twisting slightly, her gaze dropped to meet his.

"As a kid, yeah. Wanted things more exciting, but after four years of college, and traffic, and boring night skies, moving home became much more enticing."

"I feel you there."

His hand at his side, about to pull out the ring that had been burning a hole in his pocket, the hinges on the screen door squeaked open. His brother Preston had a tall glass of tea in hand and one foot on the porch when his mom's voice rang out behind him. "Preston Sweet, get back here." Caught like a deer in the headlights, Preston looked at Garret, then Jackie, and before he could advance or retreat, his mother's voice rang out again, "Preston."

"Looks like I'm needed inside." Not waiting for a third call, Preston spun around and stepped into the house, the screen door slamming behind him.

Her gaze on the door, Jackie bit back a smile and swallowed a chuckle. "Wonder what he did wrong?"

"Who said he did anything wrong?"

"I may not have known your mother very long, but there's no disguising that motherly reproving tone. All that was missing was his middle name."

"Charles." He smiled at her. "After my father."

Again the door squeaked and before his other brother could get his boot on the porch, once again, his mother called out, "Don't even think about it!"

Now Garret chuckled with no effort to hide it.

"Do you think your mother is trying to give us some privacy?"

Still grinning, he nodded. "No doubt." He figured he'd better get cracking before someone else tried to step onto the porch and his mom got laryngitis from scolding everyone. "I have something I'd like to show you."

When he pulled the box out of his pocket and flipped it open to expose the solitaire ring, her eyes widened.

"Is that what I think it is?"

He nodded. "But there's a catch."

Most people had butterflies in their stomach when they were nervous. Not Jackie. Right about now she had a flock of crazed geese swooping and diving and flapping around inside her. Her mind turned over one possibility after another, her heart holding out hope while her mind continued to churn. "Catch?"

His head bobbed again. "When we originally agreed to marry to save the ranch, I intended to give you a simple wedding band."

Somehow, she managed to nod, but words were not an option.

"Since we would need to rush through the preliminaries for a quick wedding, an engagement ring didn't make sense."

This time she couldn't even nod, her heart was hanging on every word.

"But then I saw this," Garret continued, the ring catching the silver moonlight, "and I knew it belonged on your finger."

Jackie stared at the delicate swirl of gold around the diamond, mesmerized by its simple elegance.

"The catch is," his voice softened, "I don't want our marriage to be temporary."

Her heart tripped in her chest. "What do you mean?"

Garret set the box on the railing and took both her hands in his. "I'm saying that somewhere between rescuing a drunk girl from a bar and watching you orchestrate the downfall of that jerk today, I fell in love with you. The real you."

The night air stilled around them. As if waiting for her response, the crickets seemed to pause their chorus.

"Our arrangement was supposed to be strictly business," he continued, his thumbs stroking the backs of her hands. "But every morning I wake up looking forward to seeing your smile. Every night I go to sleep thinking about the sound of your laughter. That's not business, Jackie. That's love."

A tear slipped down her cheek. "Garret…"

"When I saw you today, standing up for yourself and those other women, I realized I don't want this to end after a year. I don't want it to end—ever."

Releasing her hands, he picked up the ring box again and slowly lowered himself to one knee. The wooden porch creaked beneath him as he looked up at her, vulnerability and hope mingling in his eyes.

"Jacqueline Drake, I'm asking you—for real this time— will you marry me? Not for the ranch, not for the trust, but because I want to spend the rest of my life with you under these stars."

The world seemed to narrow to just the two of them on the porch. Through the window, she could vaguely make out shapes moving inside, but they felt distant, unimportant compared to the man kneeling before her.

"I know this is fast," he hurried on when she didn't immediately respond. "And maybe I should have waited, done this properly with candles and dinner, but—"

Finding her voice at last, she cut him off, barely managing a whisper, "Yes."

Eyes filled with disbelief blinked, a hint of a smile teased at one corner of his mouth. "Did you just say yes?"

A laugh bubbled up from deep inside her, washing away any uncertainty. "I did. To everything."

Rising to his feet, Garret tugged the ring from the box and slipped it onto her finger.

Her gaze settled on the sparkling stone, a perfect fit. A delightful surprise. What had she said not so long ago, everyone loves surprises. Slowly, she lifted her head and leveled her gaze with his. "I came to West Texas looking for a fresh start, but I found so much more. I found a home. I found you."

The hint of a smile spread wide and bright as if trying to outshine the stars. "So no more pretending?"

"No more pretending." She rose on her toes to press her lips to his.

Unlike the few short pecks on the lips for anyone looking, this kiss was just between them—it was hard and soft and sweet and strong and filled with love and passion and everything she'd ever dreamed of. A promise sealed under the vast Texas sky.

Not wanting the kiss to ever end, but knowing they had the rest of their lives to show each other the depths of their love, they slowly pulled back.

His forehead gently touched hers. "I love you, Jacqueline Drake."

"I love you more, Garret Sweet."

The two actually giggled, not moving, not wanting to lose the little contact they shared. The squeak of the porch door broke the reverie, seconds before a hard thud snapped them apart. Carson lay on the wooden porch with Preston on top of him and Jillian using one hand to stop herself from tumbling onto the pile of Sweet siblings. Behind them, Alice Sweet and her grandmother, along with the other wives and Rachel stood grinning like cats with bellies full of cream.

"I guess we had an audience." Jackie stepped back and linked her fingers with Garret's. "Good thing they could only see and not hear."

Rolling his eyes, Garret chuckled. "Good thing you said yes or I would never live this down."

His brothers scrambled to their feet and hurried into the kitchen. Righting themselves, Jillian and Rachel slapped high fives. His mom and her grandmother remained rooted to the floor, side by side, smiling happily.

"Shall we go inside and make it official?" She squeezed his fingers, delighted when he pulled her into the fold of his arms.

Heaving a slow sigh, Garret kissed her on the temple. "Ranch and trust aside, I do not want a long engagement."

She chuckled softly. "Good. Is tomorrow too soon?"

"Not for me, but I think the state of Texas won't agree. Three-day waiting period." He tugged at her hand. "Let's go inside and face the family you're going to marry into. And then I'm going to climb into bed and start counting the days until you can join me."

Her cheeks flushed hot and her gaze met his. "Me too."

Taking steps toward the house, Garret grumbled softly something that sounded like *stupid state*. She knew exactly how he felt.

EPILOGUE

Never had Rachel seen a more beautiful bride. Well, Jess and Sarah Sue had been lovely brides, but neither had been married with all the trappings. Seeing Jackie walk down the aisle of the old church with the organ playing had been breathtaking. So much so, that when she glanced at her brother, she wondered if the groom was even breathing.

Since their mother had insisted on inviting the entire town as well as every ranching friend, near or far, that she and Charlie Sweet had ever met, the only place large enough to host all those people was the old hay barn. Of course it took more work than anyone had expected to clear it out enough to fit all the rented tables.

Rachel adjusted the sky-blue bridesmaid dress, still surprised Jackie had found the perfect style of dress that looked good on her, Jillian, and Jackie's maid of honor from Houston, Katie. Scanning the surroundings, she had to admit, the transformed barn was worthy of a bridal magazine—twinkling lights draped from the rafters, wildflowers arranged in mason jars, and crisp white linens on round tables created a rustic-elegant vibe.

Her mother had finally gotten the church wedding and big reception she'd been waiting for. In only a short time, they'd pulled off an event the entire town was talking about.

"The caterers are ready for them to cut the cake," Jillian appeared at her elbow, looking flushed but happy, "and I can't find the newlyweds."

"They're over there." Lifting a finger, she pointed toward the far corner of the barn where Jackie and Garret stood, seemingly oblivious to the celebration swirling around them.

Even from this distance, Rachel could see the way Garret looked at his bride—like she was the only person in the room. His hand rested at the small of Jackie's back, his thumb tracing small circles against the delicate lace of her gown. Jackie said something that made him throw back his head and laugh, the sound carrying across the barn.

"Those two…" Jillian shook her head, smiling. "I've never seen Garret so happy."

"Seems like yesterday he was stressing about finding a suitable temporary bride." Rachel chuckled, accepting a glass of champagne from a passing waiter.

"And then she just fell into his lap. Or rather, passed out in his car."

They shared a laugh, watching as Jackie reached up to straighten Garret's tie, letting her hand linger on his chest afterward. The love-filled gesture made her smile. When he caught her fingers, pressing them to his lips in a move so tender, the sweetness made Rachel's heart squeeze.

"Guess I'll go tell the caterers to wait fifteen minutes." Jillian kept her gaze on her brother and his bride. "Those two need a little more time before we interrupt their bubble."

As Jillian disappeared into the crowd, Rachel leaned against a wooden post, observing the celebration. Her mother moved from group to group, accepting congratulations as if she were the bride herself. Eleanor Shannon chatted animatedly with Aunt Vicki near the bar, gesturing with her champagne flute. Carson and Jess swayed together on the makeshift dance floor, wrapped in each other's arms despite the upbeat tempo of the music. Preston stood, his arm around his wife, the two admiring a handmade quilt on the gift table. Somehow even that simple moment between them seemed tender and special. Her brothers had all truly hit the jackpot of love. The Sweet family marriages had started as business arrangements, but looking around now, no one would ever guess. Love had found its way in despite everyone's best efforts to keep things professional.

Rachel's gaze drifted back to Jackie and Garret. They'd moved to the edge of the dance floor, Jackie's white dress gleaming under the string lights. Garret whispered in her ear. The intensity of the way the newlyweds gazed into each other's eyes felt so personal and private that Rachel had to look away, feeling like an intruder.

Her gaze drifted back to her family. Couples. Real couples, born from the most unlikely of circumstances. The ranch, within a hair's breadth of being lost, was now slowly inching toward recovery thanks to the marriages and the trust fund initial payments. They still needed more, but at least the immediate fear of losing it all was no longer hanging over their heads by a thread. Their father would have been relieved; maybe even amused by the roundabout way they'd saved the family legacy.

She thought of Kade, still serving overseas, his absence a quiet ache amidst the celebration. They'd sent him pictures, of course, but it wasn't the same. The mantel of fully saving the ranch was now on her and Jillian. She could only hope Honeysuckle still had a few surprises left up its sleeve.

The band shifted tempo, easing into a slow, sweet country ballad. Garret led Jackie onto the floor for a proper dance, pulling her close. The barn lights seemed to dim around them, catching the sparkle of the ring on Jackie's finger as she rested her hand on Garret's shoulder. He murmured something against her hair, his smile so full of love it was almost blinding.

Rachel felt a warmth spread through her chest. The new marriage hadn't started conventionally. None of their recent marriages had. But watching her brother hold his wife as if she were the most precious, irreplaceable thing in the world, seeing the absolute certainty reflected in their eyes, she knew it didn't matter how love started. Only that it had arrived, fierce and true, right here under the Texas stars, surrounded by family.

She raised her glass in a silent toast. To Garret and Jackie. To unexpected journeys and happy landings.

Tonight she would enjoy the party and all the love surrounding them. Tomorrow, she would figure out how the heck she was going to find a husband… and fast.

Enjoy an excerpt from
Sweet Deal

E ven her mother's strong coffee wasn't quite enough to cut through the pre-dawn chill or the bone-deep weariness Rachel Sweet felt as she stood by the kitchen window. Outside, the eastern sky was just beginning to blush pink, promising another long West Texas day. A day that would start, like all the others lately, with ranch chores before the sun was fully up, followed by a full day of her real job, the one that paid her a salary, and likely more ranch chores after that. She stifled a yawn and refilled her favorite oversized mug, the one that declared 'World's Okayest Social Worker'. Some days, 'okayest' felt like a stretch.

The quiet shuffle of footsteps announced Jillian before she even appeared. Her twin eased into the kitchen, looking just as tired, her usual bright energy dimmed around the edges. She bypassed the coffee pot and went straight for the kettle.

"Tea morning?" Rachel took a long slow sip of the scalding coffee.

"Need something soothing." Jillian yawned, leaning against the counter while she waited for the water to heat. "My brain is already running through candle scent combinations and inventory spreadsheets. It's hard to switch off."

"Tell me about it." Rachel looked out the window again, past the familiar shapes of the barns and paddocks just starting to emerge from the dark. "Sometimes I dream about client files and broken fences."

"Don't forget the looming threat of foreclosure," Jillian

added dryly, pouring hot water over a tea bag in her own mug.

Rachel winced. "Way to bring down the mood before sunrise."

"Sorry." Jillian sighed, joining Rachel by the window. They stood in comfortable silence for a moment, sipping their respective drinks, the shared burden hanging unspoken between them.

Swallowing the last drop, Rachel rinsed the mug and set it in the dishwasher. "I'm heading for the barn."

Doing the same, her sister turned on her heel. "Right behind you."

Already at work mucking stalls, Garret turned to face them, his expression set with the quiet determination he seemed to wear constantly these days. "Morning."

Leaning the shovel against the wall, he straightened, stretching his back.

Rachel glanced around this side of the large barn. "Where's everyone?"

"Carson and Clint are off rounding up some cattle that broke through the east fence."

"Again?" This was the second time in as many days. Rachel knew that these things happened from time to time, sometimes more often than they'd like, but two days in a row.

"What about Preston?" Jillian asked.

"Right here." Their other brother came out of the tack room. Lately he'd taken to working on the small desk in the corner of the packed room when he didn't want to take any chance of their mom stumbling onto what they were doing to save the ranch.

"I don't like that look on your face."

"It's the only one I've got." Their brother's effort at humor fell flat.

Jillian groaned softly. "I'd like to think with three weddings in the family that we'd be in a better place, but that expression doesn't scream good news."

"No, there is some good news. Thanks to Garret's contribution," Preston's gaze darted to his brother and back, "we were able to replace the main well pump for the north pastures. No doubt it probably hadn't been maintained in years."

"Nice of it to wait till Garret and Jackie were married to finally give out." Rachel half-heartedly chuckled. "So what's the bad news?"

"While we've been able to keep up, meeting the next bank payment is going to be rough."

"I'll bite." Jillian remained focused on her brother. "How rough is rough?"

Preston blew out a long breath. "I can't make the math work."

Her brother didn't have to say what he was thinking out loud: unless one of the remaining single Sweets tied the knot. The unspoken pressure landed squarely back on her and Jillian. With Kade deployed overseas, unreachable for this kind of crazy scheme, it was down to them.

"Blast." Jillian kicked at the ground. "I've got nothing."

Rachel managed a weak smile. "Me neither. I haven't been able to find anyone even worth suggesting a temporary deal to, never mind being rejected because of the no sex clause."

Garret leaned back against the stall wall. "We need a solution, and it doesn't look like Prince Charming, even a temporary one, is riding in on a white horse anytime soon."

"I'm open to any brilliant ideas you might have." Jillian's tone dripped with sarcasm.

"Hey," Garret raised both his hands, palm open, "just stating the facts."

The weight settled heavier on her shoulders. Her brothers had stepped up, finding love in the most unexpected ways through this bizarre family pact. It had worked for them, against all odds. Now it was her turn, or Jillian's, or Kade's. She looked out at the sprawling land just beginning to wake under the Texas sky—the land that held generations of Sweet history, the land her father had loved, the land her mother was fighting so hard to keep. She couldn't let them lose it. She just couldn't.

The Pacific Ocean stretched out below, a vast expanse of improbable blue meeting an equally flawless sky. At the papparazzi's favorite restaurant for everyone who was anyone, perched high on the cliffside, the view from their table was designed to impress. A daily masterpiece served alongside pricey entrees and meticulously curated wine lists. James Henderson sipped his mineral water, the condensation beading on the delicate crystal. Everything here felt polished to a high shine, including, he was beginning to realize, the life he'd built.

Across the table, Blair adjusted the cuff of her silk blouse, the diamond on her left hand catching the California sunlight in a spray of dazzling, and very expensive, fire. She tilted her head, considering the linen swatch the wedding planner had left them. "The Egyptian cotton is lovely, of course, but I think the Belgian linen has a more... substantial feel. Speaks to legacy, tradition. Don't you agree, darling?"

Jimmy nodded, his gaze drifting past her shoulder to the endless ocean. Legacy. Tradition. Here, those words seemed to translate to thread counts and import taxes. Back home, they meant two hundred years of ranchers working the same stubborn piece of Texas land, leaky barn roofs, the taunting aroma of fresh baked goods, and the easy, unpretentious laughter shared over iced tea on the porch. He hadn't thought much about Honeysuckle in years, not really, too busy chasing the California dream. And he'd caught it. After years of late nights and long weeks, his firm thrived. Emblems of success for all to see, the sleek condo overlooking the ocean, tailored clothing suitable for a king, and the beautiful fiancée planning their six-figure wedding. He had everything he thought he ever wanted. So why did it all feel so... hollow?

"...and Henri insists that for the reception centerpieces, only white Phalaenopsis orchids flown in that morning will do. Anything less would be... well, unthinkable," Blair continued, flipping through a glossy magazine featuring impossibly thin models draped in couture. "He assures me they have a dedicated supplier."

"Sounds expensive," Jimmy murmured, forcing his attention back.

Blair waved a dismissive hand, her bracelets chiming softly. "Quality always is, darling. We can't skimp now. Think of the photos! Think of who will be there!" She leaned forward, her eyes bright with satisfaction. "Speaking of, I think seating Mother next to Judge Harrington would be a wise move, politically."

He tried to picture his own mother navigating this landscape of social maneuvering and imported orchids. She'd probably ask where the cornbread was and if the band knew "Cotton Eyed Joe." The image brought a faint, wistful smile to his lips.

"Did you hear me, James?" Blair's tone held a faint edge of impatience.

He searched for a plausible answer. "Sorry, just thinking about… logistics. Flying in orchids seems rife with potential complications."

She laughed, a light, brittle sound. "Darling, that's why we pay the best people to handle the complications." She reached across the table, her perfectly manicured nails tapping his hand. "It will be the wedding of the century. Every bride in the country will want a wedding like ours."

He had his doubts. Most people just wanted to live happily ever after with the love of their lives, regardless of whether or not the groom wore platinum cuff links. This wedding had become little more than a show. A carefully constructed statement of success and affluence, devoid of simple, genuine, even if often messy, connections mere mortals craved.

Memories of his youth flooded his thoughts. Summer nights spent cranking the ice cream machine on the front porch, laughing with friends in open fields, and swatting mosquitoes under a sky thick with stars, not city haze. The very things he'd once found boring and mundane suddenly seemed to be more full of life than the miles of ocean before them.

He looked at Blair, really looked at her. Beautiful, intelligent, ambitious—everything he thought he admired. But her focus was always outward—on appearances, status, the next acquisition. His own focus had shifted inward, questioning the very success he'd achieved. The disconnect between them felt like a chasm.

"Blair," he began softly, interrupting her rambling chatter on whether champagne or prosecco was more appropriate for the cocktail hour.

She looked up, a slight frown creasing her smooth forehead. "Yes?"

He took a breath. "I can't do this."

"Can't do what?" Her frown deepened. "Decide on the champagne? Honestly, James, sometimes you—"

"No," he cut her off. "I mean this." He gestured widely, encompassing the restaurant, the plans, the life they were building. "The wedding. Us."

Lips painted the perfect shade of notice me red formed a silent O of surprise seconds before cool eyes narrowed. "I… see. Is there someone else?" It wasn't asked with hurt, but with a kind of clinical curiosity, as if assessing a failed business deal.

"No. It's not about someone else. It's about me. This life… the one we're planning… it's beautiful, it's enviable, but it's not what I want." He sighed, his words sounding harsh to his own ears. "It's better to realize that now than years down the road." He drew the napkin from his lap and set it on the table beside him. "I'm truly sorry, Blair."

"Sorry?" Fury seemed to battle rage in her eyes, but somehow he doubted it had anything to do with a lost love and everything to do with appearances.

"What am I supposed to tell everyone?"

And there it was. Confirmation that his new reality was anything but real. Pushing to his feet and dropping cash on the table to cover the ridiculously priced water and her untouched mimosa, he looked out at the perfect blue ocean that matched his perfectly coiffed fiancée sitting at the perfectly set table. How had he ever let his life come to this?

Sweet Deal is available now

MEET CHRIS

USA TODAY Bestselling Author of dozens of contemporary novels, including the award winning Aloha Series, Chris Keniston lives in suburban Dallas with her husband, two human children, and two canine children. Though she loves her puppies equally, she admits being especially attached to her German Shepherd rescue. After all, even dogs deserve a happily ever after.

More on Chris and all her books can be found at
www.chriskeniston.com

Follow Chris' Monday Blog at her website
ChrisKenistonAuthor

Follow Chris on Facebook at
ChrisKenistonAuthor

Never miss a New Release!
Sign up for News from Chris:
www.chriskeniston.com/newsletter.html

Questions? Comments?
I would love to hear from you! You can reach me at:
chris@chriskeniston.com

www.ingramcontent.com/pod-product-compliance
Lightning Source LLC
Chambersburg PA
CBHW030006010826
48973CB00009B/2688